"Did you have to [...] by saying three li[...]

"We're not like that!" Why was Trinity mad at him?

"I know that. *You* know that. The girls weren't even insinuating something romantic."

"It just caught me off guard since we're married now."

"That doesn't change anything, Omar. You know that. We entered this for a mutually beneficial arrangement. Don't treat me like I have cooties."

"Trinity, come on. You mean to tell me it didn't surprise you?" He motioned for her to walk down the stairs.

"Of course not. I'm not falling in love again. *Ever.* And you…"

"I'm still in love with Christine."

"Exactly." She sighed, grabbing the end of one of her braids. "Sorry. I just don't want our friendship to change and it seems like it has anyway."

"Still friends?" he asked, holding out his hand.

"Yes." She slid her hand into his. "Next time just say you love me. Remember, I already know it's as a friend."

But as much as he didn't want their friendship to change…for him, it already had.

Toni Shiloh is a wife, mom and multipublished Christian contemporary romance author. She writes to bring God glory and to learn more about His goodness. A member of the American Christian Fiction Writers (ACFW) and of the Virginia Chapter, Toni loves connecting with readers via social media. You can learn more about her at tonishiloh.com.

Books by Toni Shiloh

Love Inspired

An Unlikely Proposal

Visit the Author Profile page at Harlequin.com.

An Unlikely Proposal

Toni Shiloh

LOVE INSPIRED

INSPIRATIONAL ROMANCE

LOVE INSPIRED®
INSPIRATIONAL ROMANCE

Recycling programs for this product may not exist in your area.

ISBN-13: 978-1-335-55418-5

An Unlikely Proposal

Copyright © 2021 by Toni Shiloh

This edition published by arrangement with Harlequin Books S.A.

For questions and comments about the quality of this book, please contact us at CustomerService@Harlequin.com.

Love Inspired
22 Adelaide St. West, 40th Floor
Toronto, Ontario M5H 4E3, Canada
www.Harlequin.com

Printed in U.S.A.

Whoso findeth a wife findeth a good thing,
and obtaineth favour of the Lord.
—*Proverbs* 18:22

To the Author and Finisher of my faith.

Acknowledgments

There are so many people I would love to thank for helping this book go from idea to published novel. I'd love to thank my critique partners Andrea Boyd, Jaycee Weaver and Sarah Monzon for helping me improve the many drafts of this story. You ladies are the best!

Thank you to Lana Parks for answering all my type 1 diabetes questions. I hope I did the story justice and apologize for any mistakes.

I'd love to thank the Love Inspired team. Thank you to Dina Davis for loving my first draft and believing this story had potential. Thank you to the Art team, Marketing and everyone who made my story come to life. I appreciate it more than I can say.

Last but not least, I'd like to thank my husband and kids. Glenn, thank you for listening to me talk about this story and the excitement of getting the contract. Thank you to my kids for sharing my attention with my characters. I love y'all so much!

Chapter One

"Let's get married."

Trinity Davis gaped at her best friend. "Omar, you can't be serious. I just came over to vent, not for you to suggest some harebrained idea."

Okay, not completely true. She did want a solution to her problem, but not that. Never *that*. She still had nightmares of standing in white all alone at the altar. Ever since that humiliating event—one that should have been the happiest day of her life—she'd steered clear of romance.

Besides, marriage wouldn't give her a new job. Wouldn't provide the health insurance she so desperately—

Okay, so Omar did solve that dilemma with his absurd suggestion.

"Look, Trinity. Bluebonnet is a small town. What are the odds of you finding another job here? Would you want to move away just to find one?"

She frowned, hating his sound logic.

"You can't mess around with your health. You *need* insurance." His lips turned downward, and his goatee shifted with the movement. "Your insulin has to cost a pretty penny."

Another strike for logic. "They're offering me a plan where I'd only have to pay the premiums." Being a Type 1 diabetic meant going without insulin was *not* an option. Granted, she'd almost had a heart attack at the price of the insurance.

"And how can you afford that if you have no job?"

It was like Omar could read her mind, which was certainly possible considering they'd been friends for over twenty years. "I don't know." She shrugged, trying to keep her emotions at bay. Being laid off had never entered her thoughts as a possibility. "If I want to keep paying rent, something has to give." She stuffed down a sigh as she mentally calculated her lack of income and growing expenses.

"Exactly." Omar sat back, giving the porch swing a gentle push. He sipped his sweet tea as if he'd done his job for the day and solved the world's problems.

She couldn't help but notice his skin matched the liquid gold he'd poured in the mason jars. *Focus, Trinity. What are you going to do?*

She settled into the decorative pillows on her

side of the swing. "Marriage wouldn't work, Omar."

"Why not? We're best friends. You need health insurance, and I need help with Faith and Joy. It's a solution to both of our problems."

Her heart melted. Those two girls were absolutely precious. Life hadn't been the same since Omar's wife passed away two years ago, and unfortunately, his mother-in-law, Nancy, who had been watching the girls since their mother's death, died almost two weeks ago.

Trinity looked at Omar. "Then you haven't found someone to watch the girls yet?"

"No. The home day care in town is full and the public one can't accommodate my schedule."

That made sense. His firefighter schedule of twenty-four hours on and twenty-four off made normal childcare impossible.

He twisted his tall frame, propping an arm on the back of the swing, and faced her. "If we were married, you could watch them. You'd live here so you wouldn't have to worry about rent. *And* I could add you to my health insurance, effective the day we say, 'I do.'" His lips curved. "Gotta love government insurance."

The summer's heat had dampened her skin and sweltered the back of her neck. She wrapped her braids around the ponytail holder and tucked the ends under and into a bun. *All this marriage talk is giving me hives*.

"You're awfully quiet." Omar's warm brown eyes took in her movements.

"I think it's a horrible idea." One that made her stomach drop and heave like a boat out to sea.

"I'm not Jason."

Her breath shuddered out as an image of her ex battled for front and center in her mind. She swallowed. "You're still asking me to make a commitment. To walk down a church aisle—"

"Or go to a justice of the peace courtroom."

She shook her head and continued. "Say 'I do,' and we'll...what, live happily ever after?" That only existed in movies and fairy tales.

"Are you saying a life with your best friend would be miserable?" His eyes twinkled at his attempt at humor.

He always had to make a joke, but Trinity had to admit, part of her wanted to laugh just to keep from crying. "Omar, be serious."

He slid a hand down his face and took on a serious expression. "Is this better?"

A bubble of laughter gurgled within. "You're incorrigible."

"You want serious, you got it. List the reasons why this doesn't make sense."

"People don't get married for convenience anymore."

"Ehnt."

She laughed at his imitation of a game show buzzer.

"You're so wrong. I bet if we did an internet search right now, we'd see that's not true."

She did *not* want to prove him right. "If you ever wanted to remarry—"

Omar shook his head. "Christine was it for me." His voice lowered and his gaze took on a far-off expression.

Oh, Omar. He and Christine had been perfect for each other. She remembered how in love the two had been. How could he even suggest they marry? "How can you propose, then? You loved her so much. Wouldn't anything else be a farce?"

Watching Christine decline as the cancer ravaged her body had broken Trinity's heart. She could only imagine what it had done to Omar's.

"No. We're not marrying for love, Trin. It's just a matter of convenience. Your problems would be solved by us tying the knot, and so would mine. We're adults. We can still honor vows without making a mockery of them."

"How?" she whispered. Because all she could remember was the day her intended groom failed to show up.

"By keeping God in the forefront. We'll still seek Him first. We'll raise the girls to do the same. The only question would be if you found someone to love."

"Ha." Scorn ripped the words right from her throat. "No chance of that happening." She wouldn't let it. She *refused* to let love make a fool of her twice.

"Trinity." Omar's voice coaxed her to look at him. "Not all guys are like him."

"I know that. You certainly aren't."

"See." He quirked an eyebrow. "Another reason to marry me."

She chuckled and leaned her head against his shoulder. "I love you for trying to solve my problems, but I don't think it would work."

He wrapped an arm around her and squeezed her shoulder. "Then we'll pray about it. You pray, I'll pray and God will direct us from there."

Trinity didn't want to argue with him, so she nodded. Surely God would provide for her in a different way, one that made sense and would help her walk His plan for her life. Because marrying anyone, well, that was just asinine. She'd walked down that road—*aisle*—before and had been thankful, after copious amounts of tears, to roll the dice and move off that space.

"Omar?"

"Hmm?"

"What if I have to move? I've lived here all my life."

Nowhere else compared to Bluebonnet, Texas. The vast sky that showed the wonderful colors of the sunrise or sunset. The precious bluebonnet flowers that graced the fields. And the ability to see for miles. It spoke to her heart, soothed her soul and reminded her *this* was where she was supposed to be.

"You'll handle whatever comes your way. You always have."

"But what about us? How will we keep in touch?"

"Funny thing." He paused. "There's this technology that allows you to video chat. Your face will pop up in this screen right here on my phone."

"On a phone? Get out."

His body shook with his laughter. "That's right. And my face will appear on yours."

"You're pulling my leg."

"I'll pull your hair if you're not careful."

"Ha." She sat up, moving out of his reach. "You're not in first grade anymore. That is *not* the way to get my attention."

"Hey, every boy knows that's how you get a girl to talk to you."

She rolled her eyes. "Well, use that newfangled technology now. My scalp doesn't appreciate your primitive ways."

Crinkles appeared at the corner of his eyes. "You'll be fine, Trin. God's got you."

"Thanks." She let out a breath. She would have to pray and hold on to that truth.

Omar stared at the mess that was his living room. It looked like a tornado had ripped through, leaving bits of construction paper, stuffed animals and whatnot strewn about. How did two toddlers make such a mess? His eyebrows raised as he picked a dirty diaper up off the floor.

What? How?

He was pretty sure both girls had gone to sleep with a clean diaper on. Then again, his two-year-old, Joy, liked to shed hers at the most inopportune times. The stinky offender in his hands had to be hers. He searched his memory and sighed in relief. During their nap-time battle, she'd quickly escaped her clothing and ran from him, causing the diaper to slip off. Now he could recall carting her upstairs to put on a new one before he'd tucked her in the toddler bed for a much-needed nap.

Making his way through the chaos littering his living room floor, Omar threw the diaper away in the kitchen trash can. He looked around and groaned. The mess in here was worse than the living room.

"Why, Lord? Every day is the same. They make

a colossal mess and then I clean it up." It was like a sick version of the movie *Groundhog Day*.

Maybe it had been a little selfish to invite Trinity to join his drama. Sure, she dealt with kids working at the elementary school as the librarian—or *had*, now that she'd been laid off—but they were potty-trained, coherent little beings. They didn't scream at the top of their lungs if a repulsive food item landed on their dinner plate.

Father God, I'm sorry if my proposal of marriage is out of Your will. And if it is, please give us a clear sign.

Then he would have to find another way to get the help he so desperately needed. Joy and Faith had to have supervision. Better yet, they needed love and maternal guidance. The thought of them being raised without a woman's nurturing ripped through him. If Trinity said yes, then they would be cared for, and he would have a partner who knew him and understood all his faults but called him friend regardless.

He could also keep a better eye on Trinity's health. Omar had learned to be subtle when checking on her because she didn't talk about her diabetes a lot. Ever since her diagnosis their freshman year of high school, she'd been pretty mute about her health. Why would anyone want to focus on a chronic illness? Still, he couldn't keep his concerns at bay. If they lived under the same roof, then he'd have a ladder view of her health. He could stop bugging her with the twenty questions and just enjoy her presence.

My idea is ridiculous, isn't it?

Yet, fear didn't strike him. The idea of marrying a friend brought comfort. Did that mean they should get married?

A knock interrupted his musings. He rushed to the front door and opened it, smiling at his visitor. "Hey, Rock."

His father-in-law shuffled inside, shoulders stooped a bit. "Girls napping?"

"Yes, thankfully. Can I get you something to drink?"

"A Dr Pepper if you have some. If not, I could drink some sweet tea."

"I'll grab that for you right away." Omar took a soda out of the fridge and hurried back into the living room. He handed the can over and sat across from his father-in-law. Should he tell Rock about proposing to Trinity?

It felt weird to ask Christine's father for advice, but where else would he get it? His parents had moved to Arizona in hopes the weather would be better for his father's health. His pop had more good days than bad. Omar didn't really want to bother them for advice. Of course, if he did marry Trinity, he'd tell them first. Just because they didn't live nearby didn't mean their opinions didn't hold weight. He rubbed the back of his neck.

"How's your day going?" Rock eyed him over the top of the soda can.

"Hectic."

Rock chuckled, although it sounded more like he needed to cough. "Them girls will run you ragged, I'll tell you."

"That's what I'm afraid of." He paused. "Trinity was by earlier."

"How's she doing?"

"Having a little trouble. The school won't be hiring her back come this fall."

"That's a shame." Rock's forehead lowered, making his eyes squish. "Does she have any job prospects?"

"None." And panic had filled her brown eyes. He shifted. "The public library will send someone over when the school needs assistance."

"Poor thing. I'll be praying for her." Rock took a swig of soda. "I'm surprised you don't have some scheme up your sleeve to help out."

Ha! "Interesting you should say that, Rock."

"Uh-oh. Let's hear it." Rock raised his barely-there eyebrows.

"I, uh, kind of proposed."

"Come again?"

Omar let out a nervous chuckle, relieving some of the tension. His father-in-law's opinion *really* mattered. Hopefully, Rock wouldn't think he was foolish or that he had forgotten all about Christine. "She needs health insurance, plus she won't be able to afford her place without income."

"Ri-i-ght."

"And I need help with the girls."

Sorrow filled Rock's eyes.

Omar wanted to kick himself. He knew what it was like to lose a spouse. How could he be so insensitive? "I'm sorry. I know how much you must be missing Nancy." They all missed his mother-in-law.

Rock waved a hand, though the frown lines etched across his face belied another truth. "Don't worry about it. Those girls need a lovin' hand."

"And Trinity does love them." His voice came out hesitantly. Maybe he really had been too hasty.

"'Course she does. Ain't nobody who don't love them girls." Rock tilted his head. "Y'all gonna pray about it?"

"Yes, that's what I suggested."

"Smart."

Omar's shoulders sank with relief. "How will we know it's God's will and not ours?"

"Match it with His truth." Rock rubbed his black mustache. It didn't quite match the graying beard attached to it. "My father used to tell us to pray and read the Word. Then we'd be sure to hear His still, small voice. 'Course, I didn't often listen."

"I can't picture that." Rock had always been so steady in Omar's life, and he prayed his father-in-law would be around for many years so the girls could experience his wisdom as well.

"Oh boy, I was a mess. My mama claimed I turned her head gray." He shrugged his shoulders. "Eventually I straightened out. 'Bout the time I started reading and praying just like my father said."

"So, you're saying I have some homework tonight?"

"Sure do."

"Do you think the idea's a little backward?"

"No different than seeking out a mail-order bride like they did way back when."

"But this is the twenty-first century." Not that he had a problem with it, but if he could come up with counterarguments for Trinity, then all the better.

"Mmm-hmm. Yet people use those dating sites and apps to find a person. I don't think we're so removed."

Counterpoint one. He nodded in concession. "You think it'll change our friendship?"

"It's bound to, but if that's for good or bad remains to be seen." Rock paused. "How long y'all been friends anyway?"

"My folks moved us out here when I was seven. Trinity was my first friend."

"Well, moving right next door sure helped things."

Omar smiled. "I was more interested in her tire swing than anything." It still hung in her folks' front yard, and Trinity's parents had given the girls a standing invitation to use it.

"Faith and Joy love that old swing."

"Yeah, they do." Omar steepled his fingers, hesitating to ask the question he really wanted to know. He cleared his throat. "Rock?"

"Yes?"

"Would it hurt you? To see me married to someone else?" He watched his father-in-law, hoping Rock would be honest with his answer and expression.

His eyes drooped a little. "I admit, it'll be a little uncomfortable. I expected to see you and Christine married for many years to come. But I can't begrudge you another chance at happiness. Marrying a friend…some say there's nothing better."

"I appreciate your honesty."

"Oh, you'll always get that from me, Omar." Rock stood. "I hope I'll still be welcome if you do get hitched."

"You're always welcome. You're like my second father. And you'll always be the girls' grandfather."

Rock nodded, eyes watering a bit. "I'm gonna mosey on out of here. Just wanted to say hi and hear another person's voice."

"You want to stay for dinner?" Omar glanced at his watch. "Or come back for it?"

"Might do that. But if you don't see me by five thirty, go 'head and start without me."

"All right." He followed Rock to the door and closed it quietly behind him.

Omar exhaled and looked up toward the ceiling. For all intents and purposes, Rock had given him a seal of approval. No way would he want any marriage to make Rock feel unwelcome. He was an important part of Omar's life, and Christine being gone didn't mean their status as family had been severed too.

Oh, Christine, what would you think of this?

She'd often laughed at his ideas, no matter how ludicrous they seemed. Granted, she had often egged him on to see how absurd they could become. But this was different. It was merging the lives of two people who had no desire to marry.

Jason had crushed Trinity. One day they'd been happy and in love and the next, he'd left her to pick up the pieces of her shattered heart. She'd been inconsolable.

How could Omar promise to never hurt her like that?

He straightened. *Easy.* She was his best friend and would be forever. That afforded an assurance that most people didn't have. He'd love her from that friendship and treat her with the respect she deserved as his wife and kids' stepmom.

Chapter Two

Trinity placed the traditional white dinner plate on her folks' round dining table. Her mother loved the mealtime ritual—an elegantly decorated table surrounded by her loved ones. It didn't matter if it was just the three of them or a large dinner party, her mother would pull out all the stops.

Trinity placed the cream-colored cloth napkins by each plate and finally situated the silverware on top. A vase with tulips had already been centered before Trinity had arrived. Pleased with her efforts, she walked into the kitchen.

"All done." She smiled at her mother.

"Thank you, sweetie. How's your blood sugar?"

Trinity resisted the urge to roll her eyes. You'd think her mother would realize that at the age of thirty-two Trinity was more than capable of monitoring her own health. "Mama, you know the glucometer app will sound an alert if there's a concern. The entire neighborhood will come running." She tried to keep the exasperation out of her voice.

Her continuous glucometer fed data to an app on her cell phone and max volume was the only option allowed. She didn't know why. It wasn't like the fire department needed to mistake an alert on a drop in her blood sugar for a call for help.

Trinity had removed her mother as one of her app followers in an effort to assert her independencc. Sometimes Trinity considered adding her back, but she was an adult and didn't want her mother monitoring her levels any longer.

"Right." Her mother bit her lip. "And your shot of insulin was prepared specifically for our meal?"

"Yes, Mama."

Her mother nodded, lips pressed tight as if to keep her other concerns at bay. She just needed to be distracted.

"Should I get Dad?"

"Yes, please."

The urge to yell toward the living room welled within Trinity, but she suppressed the feeling. As much as she liked teasing her mama and bending the rules—like no yelling—she just wasn't in the mood. Omar's request weighed heavily upon her heart. It was all she could think about since leaving his house earlier. Her mind kept bringing up an image of him flanked by Joy and Faith, swaying on the porch swing.

When her mother had called and invited her over for dinner, an automatic yes had flown from her lips. Trinity thought for sure she'd welcome her parents' advice, but now her hands shook as she gathered the courage to break the news. She'd been in the house for thirty minutes and hadn't used a single opportunity to talk about Omar's plan. Knowing Omar was right next door had only increased her nerves.

She stepped into the living room. "Dad, dinner's ready."

He stood, eyes glued to the TV, watching the baseball game.

"Dad?"

"I'll be in as soon as a commercial comes on." His husky voice practically shooed her away.

She suppressed a chortle. "Okay." She chuckled softly as she entered the dining room.

"He's waiting for a commercial, isn't he?" Her mom placed a hand on her hip.

"Sure is."

They laughed as they sat down at the oak table, the same one she'd eaten dinners at as a kid. Nothing in their home ever changed unless broken beyond repair. After a minute, her father shuffled in, pushing the saloon-style doors on their hinges.

He dropped into his chair. "The Rangers are killing me. They let the Astros load the bases." He shook his head in disgust.

"It's the third inning, Dad. Game's not over yet."

"It will be if they continue playing that way. But I'll hush so we can say grace." He placed his arms out, palms up.

Trinity reached for his hand and then her mother's. Her father said grace, and after a chorus of amens, they began eating. The familiarity of meat loaf, mashed potatoes and cabbage calmed her. After a few bites, the silence begged to be broken.

"I saw Omar today."

"How's he doing?" Her mom studied Trinity, her brow creased with sympathy.

"I think he's still hurting. A little lost maybe?" *More like desperate.* How bad off did one have to be to suggest a marriage of convenience? With Trinity, no less.

"Grief will do that to you."

Trinity bit her lip. It was true, she could see how much his mother-in-law's death hurt him and the girls. Not to mention the grief that still lingered from Christine's passing. But did that mean she had to go along with this silly idea?

You wouldn't have to worry about money or in-surance anymore.

"I saw Rock leaving earlier. Was he there too?" Her dad shoved in a forkful.

Oh no! How would he feel if they married? Trinity refocused on her dad. "No. He probably came over after I left."

"I wonder who will watch those precious girls now." Her mother dabbed at her mouth in all her Texas refinement.

A shudder spread chill bumps along Trinity's arms. "Well…" She twirled her fork back and forth. "Omar suggested I could help." *Not exactly how he'd phrased it.*

"What do you mean?" Her dad paused, fork in midair.

"He, uh…" Why was her heart pounding so fast? Could it beat its way out of her chest? "He asked me to marry him."

Forks clattered.

Tension filled the room.

Trinity slowly turned to look at her mom, whose mouth had dropped open. She then looked to her dad. If he squinted his eyes any tighter— well, he might as well close them.

She carefully placed her fork alongside her plate, then clenched the fabric of her skirt. "Y'all, please say something. Mama? Dad?" *Somebody!*

"That sounds a bit extreme, don't you think?

Not the first idea that comes to mind for solving childcare woes." Her mother clutched her navy blue costume necklace.

If they had been pearls, Trinity would have lost all composure. "I figured."

"He has heard of a babysitter, right?" Her dad quirked a silver-colored eyebrow. She'd always thought it looked distinguished against his brown skin.

Trinity didn't know whether to laugh or cry. "He has, but it's kind of hard to find someone who can accommodate the fire department's twenty-four-hour shifts."

"So, he wants you to just toss aside your whole life to accommodate his schedule?" Her dad's voice lowered dangerously.

She hated when he talked like that. Knowing his anger was directed at Omar didn't make Trinity feel any less like a kid awaiting disciplinary actions. "It actually started because of my job."

Her dad leaned back in his seat, arms crossed and jaw clenched.

"Since I need health insurance—"

"Oh, honestly." Her mom waved a hand in the air. "Trinity, you can't marry that man to have some insurance and raise his girls as some kind of quid pro quo."

"But where am I going to find another job, Mama? And one with good insurance?" She shook her head. How had she ended up defending Omar's reasons? Hadn't she thought the idea was too absurd for words? "Anyway—" she exhaled "—I don't think he's thinking too clearly. I mean, his mother-in-law just passed away not two weeks ago. He's simply a little panicked." *But he spoke so clearly.*

No panic. No desperation.

A friend helping a friend. She bit back a groan.

"I don't care." Her father slapped his napkin down on the table.

"Charles," her mom snapped. "The boy's been walking in a cloud of grief since his wife died. Now Nancy. Have a little sympathy."

Wait. Now her mother was jumping onto the sympathy train? Trinity placed a hand on her head, hoping the room would right itself and make sense. There was too much flip-flopping around.

"She's my baby girl. I have to look out for her best interest," her father protested.

"Yes, but she can make her own decisions."

Trinity snorted. Yet her mother had just been eyeing her insulin pod and treating her like it was the first day of her Type 1 diabetes diagnosis. She gripped the table. "You know what? I completely agree. I'm more than capable of making my own decisions. Only this time, I really need your opinions and advice. This isn't me deciding on the color of a car. This is major." Her breath came in spurts as her panic levels rose like a spike in her glucose readings.

Now wasn't the time for them to decide they had no opinion. Her dad's bluster wasn't exactly helping the mounting anxiety turning her hands clammy.

Her father reached for her hand, understanding softening the glare in his eyes. "Baby girl, you know you can tell him no, right?"

"Of course." But she'd also promised Omar she'd pray about it. Talking to her parents was a step in the wise counsel direction.

"What are you thinking?" her mother asked.

"I'm not quite sure. It seems a little ridiculous…" Her voice trailed off.

"But you're liking the insurance idea, huh?" Her dad's expression was contemplative.

"I need it, Dad. What if I run out of insulin before I get more insurance? How will I pay for it?" Her copay with insurance made her queasy, and she could only imagine the amount without it.

"Oh, sweetie." Her mother leaned toward Trinity and cupped her cheek. "God always provides."

"And what if Omar's His provision?"

Her mother gaped and her father jerked. Even Trinity was surprised by the words out of her mouth.

"You may have a point, baby girl." Her father stroked his chin.

"Charles, I can't believe you'd say something like that. I thought you were against this." Her mom blinked owlishly.

"I was until I started thinking about it. Think, Rhonda, they'll both be helping each other out."

"But what about love?" her mother cried.

Trinity watched in amusement. "You know I have no desire to put myself in that position again, right?"

"Oh, Trinity, Jason was a jerk." Her mother covered her mouth. "Forgive me, Lord."

"Hey, it's true." Her father smiled.

Trinity chuckled. "Y'all, seriously. Neither one of us wants to marry, but this way we can help one another. And share each other's burdens. Right?" The more she talked about it, the less outrageous the idea seemed.

"I don't like this." Her mother stabbed her meat loaf, shaking her head. "You could fall in love with someone, have a family. But if you marry Omar, that's for life, young lady."

She nodded. "I know." Her beliefs wouldn't let her take marriage lightly.

"And you know nothing about toddlers. It's like throwing a person who can't swim in the deep end of a pool," her mother continued.

"But she'll learn to swim," her father countered.

"Humph. Or sink." Her mother shook her head.

A light sparkled in her dad's eyes. "Wait a minute, you'd be a stay-at-home mom for the next couple of years?" At her nod, her dad threw his head back and laughed.

"Hey! What's that supposed to mean?" She couldn't help the hurt in her voice. Whatever her father was thinking probably wasn't a good thing.

"Baby girl, you like control. Those little girls are going to turn your world upside down and ruin your love of order."

"I'm sure I can get them on a schedule."

Her mother snorted. "Right. Because kids will do whatever you tell them a hundred percent of the time." Her mother sent a pointed look Trinity's way.

A different kind of nervousness weighed on her shoulders. All this time she'd been focused on her heart and avoiding the institution that had nearly destroyed her before, but what about Faith and Joy? Would this scar them? Would she be a good mom?

"What do I do?" she whispered.

"Pray," her parents said in unison.

Her mom looked at her dad knowingly. "It's the only thing you can do right now, sweetie."

"I'm surprised Omar didn't do so or even suggest it." Her father eyed her.

"He did."

"Hmm." A glimmer of respect shone in her father's eyes. "We'll pray for y'all too."

"Thank you, Dad."

"Of course, baby girl."

The rest of their meal centered on lighter conversation, but Trinity couldn't entirely focus. She couldn't help but feel like her life would drastically change with an answer to Omar. Whether it was yes or no, their relationship would be altered forever. Could it withstand a yes? Or worse, a no?

Hot tears pricked her eyes, waiting to be shed, but she couldn't let her parents see how unnerved she truly was. Agreeing to marry another person after what had happened before…

Trinity gave a mental shake of the head. Marriage to Omar wasn't something she wanted to entertain, but the idea held so many pros. Plus, there was no risk of her heart being engaged. In a way, it was like a safety net that would protect her from the pain of love.

The irony of it all.

Omar gave a sigh of thanks. *Sunday.*

Going to church always centered him. For a couple of hours, his troubles would fade away as he worshipped and remembered Who had ultimate control.

Yet today was bound to be awkward. He hadn't spoken to Trinity since he popped the question, mostly because he wanted to give her time to process. Except now he had to break that silence. They'd been going to church together since they were kids. Well, except for the few years he'd been married to Christine. Trinity had sat near them at church but never with them—respecting their family time, as she'd claimed. When Christine passed away, Trinity had taken to sitting with him once more in a demonstration of comfort and friendship.

Which is why he stood outside her apartment door waiting for her to answer his knock.

The door swung open and Trinity stood there, a slew of bobby pins hanging from her lips. "Just a moment," she mumbled, as her hands twisted her braids into a contorted updo.

Amazing what she could do with some bobby pins. With deft fingers, she glided the final one in place while sliding her feet into heels. She grabbed a cardigan and her Bible, and a smile lit up her beautiful dark brown face. "Ready."

He chuckled. "Running a little late this morning?"

"I hit snooze too many times."

"I am *not* surprised." He guided her down the stairs, thankful that their conversation was light. It seemed normal. Guess he hadn't ruined everything with his suggestion.

Omar opened the passenger door, shutting it after Trinity settled into the seat. If they got married, Sunday mornings would pretty much be the same, except he wouldn't have to drive to her apartment to pick her up anymore. She'd already be in his house.

The thought drew him up short. Was he ready to have another woman there? Another wife?

Your relationship with Trinity isn't like that.

True. He didn't need to get worked up over nothing.

When he opened the driver's door, singing greeted him. He raised his eyebrows at Trinity as he slid in. She shrugged, a slight smile on her face, and continued to sing "Amazing Grace" with Faith and Joy. Faith held out the last note and then exhaled when finished.

"Bravo." He patted his leg to clap while holding on to the wheel with his other hand and turning out of the parking lot. "What brought that on?"

"I wanted to sing for Miss T. She said we all sing," Faith pronounced.

"Y'all did a beautiful job."

Faith beamed and Joy giggled.

The singing continued all the way to church. As he parked a couple of rows away from the front entrance, the girls ended their last song. "Daddy, you sing next time."

Trinity laughed. "You know he can't sing, right?"

"Hey." But his protest was in half jest. He was

tone deaf, much to the chagrin of everyone who had the unfortunate opportunity of hearing him sing.

"God loves all singing."

Trinity sighed, placing a hand over her heart. "You're right, Faith. Thank you for that beautiful reminder."

The three-year-old nodded primly as if she knew she'd been right all along. Omar stifled a chuckle.

He and Trinity got out of the vehicle, then opened the back doors, each helping one of the girls from their car seats. As they walked into the building, Omar was struck by the image they made. How had he not noticed the family picture they projected every Sunday? He held Faith's hand while Trinity clasped Joy's and the girls grabbed each other's free hand.

All of them connected like a real family.

Omar *knew* they could do this—provide a home full of love, laughter and, apparently, singing. He wanted to plead with Trinity to say yes. The more he thought about the arrangement, the more right a yes felt. However, if he pushed the subject, would Trinity run the other way? He sighed. All he could do was ramp up his prayers and plead to the One who could make a difference.

After dropping the girls off in the toddler room, he and Trinity headed to the sanctuary.

Trinity placed a hand on his arm as they stood before the sanctuary. "Omar, could we talk later?"

His heart thudded. "Sure. Is it about…?"

"Yes." She nodded. "I had some questions before I give you an answer."

"Okay." *What are they?* he wanted to ask, but the worship music started.

Trinity always liked to hear all of the songs in their entirety, so he led her to their usual spot. He would have to be patient and wait until church was over. Hopefully Rock could watch the girls after church, so Omar could talk with Trinity.

He scanned the seats, searching for his father-in-law, but couldn't find him in his usual spot. *Lord God, I pray that he's okay. Please comfort Rock as he grieves. I pray for the wisdom to know what to do or say.*

Maybe he'd invite Rock over for dinner again. He hadn't shown up the last few times, but that didn't mean Omar had to stop asking. *Also, Lord, could You help me and Trinity navigate the marriage talk?* It was so odd to pray that, let alone think it.

A friend loveth at all times.

The scripture came to mind as he stood there with his best friend. Is that what he was doing? If so, then maybe marrying wasn't such a bad idea.

Chapter Three

Returning to the scene of the crime.

Trinity couldn't help the thought as she took a spot on Omar's porch swing. When she'd asked to talk about the proposal, her mind had been on the logistics of it all. But now, the only thought in her mind was of them sitting here as a family.

Was she overthinking this? Maybe Omar had no intention of being a real family, but simply had a roommate lifestyle in mind. One where they kept their own bank accounts but split financial burdens.

But you don't have a job anymore.

"Ugh," she muttered. How did she keep forgetting that little factoid?

"Sorry about that." Omar jogged up the front steps, pausing on the wooden landing. "Had to drop the girls off at Rock's real quick." He hooked a thumb toward his front door. "You need something to drink?"

"Bottled water, please."

"Coming right up." He dashed inside and moments later charged out with a Dr Pepper and bottled water.

After handing her the bottle, Omar sat down and popped the top on his soda. "So."

"So," she drawled.

"It doesn't have to be awkward."

"Ha. My best friend asked me to marry him with no love involved. Pretty sure that's the definition of awkward."

"Or the resourcefulness of a genius at work."

She chuckled, pushing his arm slightly in amusement.

"Seriously though," he looked at her, "what are your thoughts? Other than you considering my plan slightly wacky?" He waggled his eyebrows Groucho Marx–style.

"It's not *that* bad. I have to admit, after talking to my parents—"

He groaned, dropping his head back before meeting her gaze once more. "Is that why your mom kept squinting her eyes at me during service?"

"Yes."

"But I thought she loved me?" He put on a

wounded look, the corner of his eyes turning downward to add punch to the look.

Omar was a hoot. "Not right now, she doesn't."

His lips joined in the game, the bottom one poking out.

"You look like Faith."

"I sincerely hope not." He laughed. "I wouldn't wish my looks on those girls any day of the week."

"Please, you know you're handsome."

"Really?" He arched an eyebrow. "I don't think you ever paid me such a compliment, Trinity Davis."

She rolled her eyes. "Just because I don't fawn over you like some people, doesn't mean I can't admire the even symmetry of your face."

"What?" he asked on a chuckle. "Is that what women look for? Eyes that line up?"

"Maybe subconsciously." He really was handsome. She never made a big deal of it since all the single women in Bluebonnet did that for her. It didn't help that his fit figure was usually covered by a Bluebonnet Fire Department uniform. The navy blue contrasted well with his brown skin.

"All right. Enough flattery—what do you want to know?"

She rolled her eyes. "How is this supposed to work? Are you expecting a wedding where we invite friends and family?"

Just the thought of wearing a wedding dress made her itch. She tightened her grip around the water so she wouldn't be tempted to scratch at the nonexistent rash.

"Honestly, I figured we'd go to the justice of the peace, sign the certificate and come back home." He cleared his throat. "Here. I was thinking you could have the guest room."

"What if you have guests?"

"Right. My parents are always visiting." He gave her an *are-you-kidding-me* expression.

"Don't be smart." She shook her head. "What if I have guests?"

"You have any other friends besides me and Jalissa?"

Yikes! How had she forgotten to consult her other best friend? Granted, Jalissa was five feet of snark and biting sarcasm. She'd probably lecture Trinity on stupid decisions and their consequences. No, she really didn't want Jalissa's opinion on marriage right now. She'd bring up the hurt Trinity had experienced after being jilted as a reminder to not be swayed. Trinity's memory was just fine without Jalissa's input.

"You're right. I can sleep in the guest bedroom." She bit her lip. "I can't contribute to utilities right now. I mean, I have a little saved up—".

Omar held up a hand. "Don't worry about it. It'll be a little tight until we find our footing."

"What if I can get a job that allows me to work from home?"

Omar smirked. "Yeah, you may not think that's feasible after spending the day with the girls."

Why did everyone make it sound like she had no experience with children? She'd been the school librarian, surrounded by kids on a daily basis. Plus, like every teen in Bluebonnet, she'd done her share of babysitting back in high school. Granted, that had been over a decade ago, but still.

"I'm sure I can handle them." She was smart. Capable, even. Not to mention, the girls loved her.

"Of course you can, but there are days they'll test your limits." Omar shifted his leg, and the swing swayed with the movement. "So, we've figured out housing, finances—"

"Wait. We didn't figure out finances. I need to do *something* to contribute."

"You are. Watching the girls is a necessity I can't afford. You're saving me money in that regard."

"It's not enough." She didn't want this to be some lopsided arrangement.

"Fine. Look for a job, but if you can't find something, it really won't be a problem." He stared at her pointedly.

"Thank you."

"Any other questions?"

"What are we going to tell the girls? Am I acting as their nanny or step—" She couldn't say the word. She had no idea how he'd react if she said the one label that animated movies had been telling children was always preceded with a *wicked*.

Omar sighed. "I'm not sure how much they understand about weddings and whatnot. We'll explain it to them after the ceremony. And if they don't understand, we'll just say you'll be moving in and living in the house."

"Okay." It wasn't a perfect answer but completely understandable. "And we're both in this for life, right?" She couldn't divorce. Even if she was jumping into a marriage for the convenience of it all, she still believed in the long-lasting vows.

"Right. The Bible's pretty clear on that. Besides, I don't think a lot of couples in the Bible married for love."

"True." Did Boaz love Ruth? She'd like to think so. He seemed so upstanding.

"Then that's it? We're getting married?" Omar's brown eyes watched her expectantly.

She hesitated, words perched on the tip of her tongue. "I… I guess so."

"It'll be okay. You'll see." He wrapped her in a side hug, squeezing her arm.

"I hope so, Omar. I'd hate to mess up our friendship over health insurance and childcare." Trinity choked out a laugh she didn't really feel.

"You won't. *We* won't. It's bound to feel strange at first, but I'm sure we'll get into a rhythm. Our relationship has always been easy."

"You're right." She squeezed her eyes shut. Why was she so worried?

Being Omar's friend came as naturally as breathing air. From the moment she'd seen the quiet seven-year-old staring at her tire swing, she'd known they'd be friends. They had swung from the old tree in her parents' yard until both of their parents had come outside and called them in. The next day, Omar had showed up the moment she'd sat on the tire swing, kind of materializing out of thin air. It had scared her and made him laugh. They'd been forever friends ever since.

"Thank you for this. I can't tell you how much I appreciate your friendship. That you'd help me out by marrying me." Her stomach rolled. She'd have to figure out how to say the word without nausea taking over.

"Hey, friends help each other out."

"When should we tie the knot, so to speak?" Her breath shuddered out.

She'd never imagined setting another wedding date. *Never.* Would Omar be offended if she showed up at the courthouse with a rash of hives all over? The image was so comical she snorted out loud.

"What?"

Trinity told him what she was thinking.

"Hey, I'm not *him*. I'll be there, bright and early, and ready to say 'I do.'"

"How about we promise if the other doesn't show up, no hard feelings. It's a big thing to commit to."

"I'm not Jason, Trin."

"I know, Omar." For one they didn't look alike. Jason had been a lighter shade than Omar, although both of them were African American. Besides, her ex had hightailed it out of Bluebonnet before she even knew what happened while Omar was always there for her.

Always.

Omar pulled out his cell phone and clicked on his calendar icon. "How about June seventh? It's my last day off."

And summer had already started for her, so Trinity had nothing preventing her from showing up. It's not like they needed to marry on a Saturday or anything. She gave a nod. "The seventh it is."

The day would forever be imprinted on his mind and his life. Omar swallowed, pushing down the urge to glance at his watch once more. Trinity had decided to ride with her parents to the courthouse. She'd already moved all of her things into the guest room yesterday. Or rather, he had, with the help of Mr. Davis and Rock.

Mr. Davis. He'd asked Omar to call him Charles, but it felt weird, wrong even. He'd been calling Trinity's dad Mr. Davis since he moved to Bluebonnet. To be able to call him Charles simply because he was marrying the man's daughter unnerved Omar a bit.

Okay, more like a lot, Lord. I'm going out of my mind. Maybe Trinity had the right idea about backing out.

Not that she had said that, per se. More like there would be no hard feelings. Judging by the tangled knots in his stomach, he'd rather face a five-alarm fire than…

Than what? Marry your best friend?

A friend loveth at all times.

Again, that verse rolled in his mind. He *did* love Trinity. As a friend. She was the steadiest person in his life. Without her, he'd have fallen apart after Christine's death. Christine's absence had left a giant hole in his life and Trinity had been there to help him navigate through it all. He couldn't fail her.

When he'd called his parents, they'd been shocked but happy—until he told them it was simply for convenience. His mom had been disappointed. Apparently, she'd always thought he'd marry Trinity. Since they couldn't fly out to attend the ceremony, they'd offered the use of his paternal grandmother's wedding ring. And since Christine had worn his grandmother's ring on his mom's side, it seemed right for Trinity to have something of his family as well.

Before he could take a step toward the door, it opened.

Trinity strolled through wearing a red polka-dotted dress. Her braids hung freely down her back, pulled back by a red headband. Her dark brown skin glowed beneath the florescent lights and blush colored her cheeks. He was pretty sure the color was due to cosmetics and not a natural response on her part.

He couldn't help the slight catch of his breath at how pretty she looked. She rarely wore dresses, preferring skirts that fell to her ankles and jeans with long tops. This dress stopped at her knees and she wore those weird sandals where the straps tied around her lower leg.

"Hey." He smiled, stepping forward. "You look pretty." *Ugh.* Did that sound as awkward to her ears as it did to his?

"And I didn't yesterday?"

"What? No. I mean, yes." He stopped, as Trinity gave in to the mirth. Omar shook his head. "Should have known you'd tease me."

"Can't pass on the opportunity."

He smiled. "So, are we good?" he asked, lowering his voice. Hopefully her parents couldn't hear him.

"*I* am." Her dark eyes met his. "Are you?"

Was he? The nerves from earlier had all but disappeared with her presence. He did a mental assessment then nodded. "I'm ready."

Relief brought her twin dimples out. "Great. Is the judge ready for us?"

"Not yet. I think he was waiting on the bride." He winked, hoping to pull a chuckle from her.

Trinity could take forever to get ready. He knew she had to set her alarm two hours before church just to be ready for when he'd arrive. And still, she was always in midpreparation when he showed up. Why should their wedding day be any different?

"Omar Young, is your party complete?" Mrs. Whitam, the court secretary and receptionist, called to him from behind the partition.

"Yes, ma'am."

"All right. Let me let y'all in."

She left the partition and quickly appeared behind the glass door leading to the courtrooms. "Judge Hanvoy will marry y'all in room three." She looked at them appraisingly. "I always knew y'all would marry. I told Harry, 'Mark my words, those two will be married forever.'"

"Uh…thanks?" He knew most of the folks in Bluebonnet expected him to marry Trinity, but

Christine had been it for him. One look at her caramel skin and bright sunny smile, and he'd been a goner.

"Of course, Omar. I'm happy your girls will have a woman in the house. You would have gone completely gray as a single father. My Harry always says I'm the reason he still has pepper in his hair."

Trinity shook beside him, probably trying not to laugh at Mrs. Whitam's antics.

They walked to room three and entered. Mrs. Whitam wished them "all the best" and left them waiting. Trinity's parents took the first row of seats in the gallery. Omar looked around, wondering what to do. He slid his hands into his pockets.

He'd worn a tuxedo the first time he married but Trinity hadn't wanted to dress up today, so he'd thrown on his dress uniform. It was better than jeans and less formal than a tux. At least, that had been his way of thinking. He couldn't help but notice how his uniform complemented her red dress.

Finally, Judge Hanvoy walked in, looking down at his paperwork. He halted and slowly gazed up, doing a double take. "I thought I read the wrong names."

Omar chuckled. "No, that's right." He assumed the judge held their marriage license, which Omar had given Mrs. Whitam earlier.

Judge Hanvoy walked over to the middle of the courtroom and motioned them to join him on the other side of the partition. "Is there something y'all want to tell me?"

"Uh…" Omar looked at Trinity. Seemed like the people of Bluebonnet didn't know how to act about their marriage.

She shrugged.

"I wasn't aware you two had been dating."

Omar's gut clenched. "As you know, we're best friends." His hands curled into a fist, hidden by his pockets.

"I know, but when did y'all graduate to more?"

They hadn't, and he had no plans to go that direction. Just a mutually beneficial marriage with friendship and respect. Most married couples could only hope for those things, right? The kind of love he'd had with Christine didn't happen twice in a lifetime.

He pulled himself from his musings. "With all due respect, sir, does that matter?"

"I take the sanctity of marriage seriously, Mr. Young. Just because we're in a courthouse and not a church doesn't mean the Lord's not watching."

"We understand that, sir. We've discussed it, and we're not here to play games."

The judge stared at Omar and then turned his unwavering gaze on to Trinity. Omar wanted to sigh in relief now that the judge's hawk eyes were off of him. He could sense Trinity trying not to fidget.

Judge Hanvoy must have come to some conclusion because he placed the paperwork down and spoke to them. "Very well, then. Join hands and repeat after me."

Omar held his hands out, offering them to Trinity who slid hers against his palms. His heart pounded as his mind pulled up two different ceremonies—a bride in a glorious white dress and one wearing red with white polka dots.

Lord God, please help me focus on the woman before me. I don't want to tarnish Christine's memory or disrespect Trinity.

He looked deep into Trinity's eyes as she pulled a ring out of her dress pocket and posed it over his ring finger.

"I, Trinity Davis, take you, Omar Young, for my lawfully wedded husband." Her voice shook as she continued. "To have and to hold from this day forward, for better, for worse, for richer, for poorer, in sickness and health, until death do us part."

He glanced down, noting with surprise the black-and-red silicone wedding ring. It was the kind he could wear on the job and not worry about any complications from wearing metal. Trust a friend to put thought into his ring. He pulled her wedding ring his mom had shipped him overnight out of his pocket. The three stones sparkled in their simplicity.

As he spoke his vows, he fought memories of hospital visits and graveyard sites. A bead of sweat rolled down his spine. Finally, he slid the ring onto Trinity's finger. *Trinity, not Christine.*

"I now pronounce y'all husband and wife." Judge Hanvoy took out a pen and signed the certificate with a flourish. "Y'all sign above the husband and wife spaces. Trinity, your parents can sign as witnesses."

"Yes, sir."

Omar passed the pen to Trinity, who signed and passed it to her father. He looked down at his left hand. It was done. They were married and officially husband and wife.

Now what?

Chapter Four

Trinity stared at the red-roofed, two-story farm-house. The white siding needed repair, but the black shutters framing the windows appeared sturdy. It had an aged look that was more welcoming than dilapidated. The front porch and its swing were her favorites. Maybe she could add a small table and a couple of chairs for the girls on the portion of the porch that wrapped around to the side.

Don't get ahead of yourself.

All of her stuff had been placed in the guest bedroom—*her* room—last night. The other items that couldn't fit had been given away to the church. Trinity had to remember she couldn't just move in and put her stamp on things right away. It would be pretentious, domineering, and...

She didn't know what else. Just knew she couldn't steamroll Omar, despite feeling like an outsider taking up residence in a place that had no room for her. Which was ridiculous. This was her best friend, and she already knew the girls. *You're not an outsider.* She forced herself to move toward the porch steps.

Omar had already climbed them and waited for her at the top. If he thought she was going to let him carry her over the threshold, he had another think coming. Thankfully, he simply held out his hand when she made it to the last step.

"You ready?"

"For what?" She gave him the side-eye. *Do not pick me up.*

"Family life." He winked and waggled his hand, reminding her she'd left him hanging.

She placed her palm against his, and he squeezed her hand in return.

"We've got this, Trin."

"Right. Nothing abnormal about the past few hours."

"Hey, everyone thought we'd marry at some point anyway, right?"

She didn't know whether to laugh or shake her head in bemusement. She went with a tight-lipped smile.

Omar stopped, turning to face her and took her other hand. "Hey. We're best friends, remember?"

"I remember." She stared at the light brown flecks in his eyes. Same Omar, but everything else had changed. "It's just that this is kind of weird."

"It will be if we let it. We're going to go in there, hang out with the girls and maybe play some Mario Kart."

"You mean you'll lose to me."

He chuckled. "Exactly. A normal day, only you won't have to leave anymore."

"All right." She exhaled. "Just an everyday sort of day."

"Right." He squeezed her hands once more and then opened the screen door before heading inside.

"Daddy!" Faith squealed, pumping her little legs to get to him.

Joy followed, trying her best to catch up.

Trinity wanted to chuckle at them, but she was too delighted. The love between those three warmed her heart. Omar bent, swinging Faith up into his arms and tossing her a little above his head. He caught her, kissed her cheek and set her back down. Then he repeated the greeting with Joy.

"Miss Trinity." Faith held her arms over her head in the universal motion of wanting to be picked up.

She scooped Faith up, inhaling the baby body-wash scent. Faith wore two braided pigtails that had seen better days. Guess that was one duty she could take over. She'd always loved braiding hair and didn't have any sisters to do it on. Every doll she'd owned growing up had been to her pretend beauty shop.

"Are you here to play with us?" Faith's obsidian eyes watched her.

Trinity looked at Omar, waiting for his lead. Rock had taken the girls to the park yesterday so she could move all her things into the guest room. Part of her believed they should have told the girls before the wedding, but then again, if one of them hadn't shown up today that would have raised a lot more questions.

"Girls, let's sit down," Omar suggested.

Faith wiggled, signaling she wanted to walk, so Trinity put her down. They all sat on the couch.

Omar met Trinity's gaze then studied his daughters. "Miss Trinity is going to live with us from now on."

"Why?" Faith's eyes darted back and forth between Trinity and Omar.

"Well, we got married today."

"Ma-weed?" Joy repeated, her grin showcasing her baby teeth.

Faith tugged on his arm. "Daddy, what's married?"

Omar's mouth formed into a small O. Trinity would have laughed if nerves hadn't rendered her mute.

"Uh, well, baby, it's when a man and a woman care about each other and want to live together to raise a family."

Faith's brow wrinkled and she turned her gaze toward Trinity. "Trinity is our family?"

Trinity's heart turned over. She always wanted a family. Although she and Omar had taken an unconventional route, this made the nerves of earlier worth it. These girls needed a mother. "I am. Would you like to be family with me?"

The girls' heads bobbed in unison, and she smiled.

"Good," Omar stated, "because now Trinity's my wife and your stepmom."

"Stepmom?" Joy parroted.

Faith jerked her head up, her eyes wide as she stared at them. "Like a mommy? A not-in-heaven mommy?"

Tears sprang to Trinity's eyes. She hugged Faith to her side and squeezed Joy's hands. She looked toward Omar, wondering how he was handling all of this.

He slowly nodded. "Yes, Faith."

"Yay." She clapped and turned to Trinity. "Let's have tea parties."

"Of course." Trinity smiled at the girls. "But right now, do you want to make a cake? I could use a helper."

"What kind?" Faith's little face scrunched up in consideration.

"Chocolate?"

"'Kay. I help."

"Me too." Joy tugged on Trinity's dress.

"Of course, you too." She stood and picked Joy up, sliding the little girl onto her hip. "Wow, you're getting big."

"Me too, Miss Trinity."

She hoisted Faith up and stilled, making sure she had a good hold on both of them before moving. "I don't know if I can walk." She exaggerated her movements, pretending to struggle as she slowly walked toward the kitchen.

Their giggles filled her ears. Such a sweet sound. She continued her slow movements until she reached the kitchen doorway where Rock stood. While Trinity and Omar had been at the courthouse, Rock had watched the girls. He'd probably even watched their moment in the living room just now. Her throat sounded out a hello, the word swallowed up by the girls' laughter.

Rock gave Faith and Joy a slow smile before dipping his head Trinity's way. "Everything went well this morning?"

"It did." She gulped, trying to push down the apprehension slithering up the back of her neck. Would he resent her presence in Omar's home? Think she was encroaching on Christine's territory? What had he thought about the conversation she and Omar had just had with the kids?

"I'm glad to hear that. Those little girls need some mothering." His voice choked at the end.

Trinity's heart dropped to her feet. She set the girls down and took his hands in hers. "I promise to do right by them, Rock. *All* of them."

He sniffed, eyes watering a bit. "I know you will, Miss Trinity. You've always been a good friend to Omar and my sweet Chris." He patted her hand. "Love them with all the good Lord gives you and you'll be just fine."

Now it was her turn to get a little teary-eyed. She nodded as she took a moment to get her emotions under control. "You're staying for dinner, aren't you?"

"Nah. Don't let this old man get in your way." He pushed off the door frame. "Y'all need to find your footin' before inviting me into the mix."

"You're always welcome here, Rock," Omar said, coming to stand by her side.

"My thoughts exactly," she chimed in. She would never run the girls' grandfather off.

Besides, she'd always had a warm spot in her heart for Rock. He had lots of wisdom to offer if a person took a moment to talk to him.

"I appreciate that, but I need to be alone right now."

Omar's gaze darkened, but he nodded in understanding.

Trinity wished she knew what to do. Both men had an intimacy with grief she wasn't privy to. It left her feeling inadequate. What did you say to a person who'd lost their spouse? The one they'd pledged their life to until death. *I'm sorry for your loss* seemed so insufficient in the face of such heartache.

"Miss T, cake!" Joy tugged on her hand, pulling her toward the kitchen.

"Excuse me, gentlemen. Cake baking awaits."

Rock dipped his head in acknowledgment while Omar simply smiled.

She followed the girls into the kitchen. The floor plan had an old school feel with an eat-in kitchen to the right and the actual cooking space to the left. A small square table with two of the chairs outfitted with child's seats completed the dining area.

She looked around the kitchen counter, searching for step stools. *Nothing.*

"Whatcha looking for?" Faith eyed her curiously.

"A step stool. Do y'all have those?"

The girls shook their heads. Joy clutched a small blanket that had a bunny head to her chest. It was cute but rather worn.

"I suppose we'll have to mix everything at the table then."

Once she strapped the girls into their high-chair booster seats, Trinity filled the table with measuring cups and supplies to make the cake. She'd added her personal groceries to Omar's fridge and pantry yesterday. He didn't have a lot of the staples she used in her daily diet.

Trinity tried not to eat so stringently that she left no room to enjoy life, but she couldn't deny the modifications necessary for a Type 1 diabetic. Avoiding excessive sugar and heavy carbs were a must, but she also left room for the occasional splurge like today's chocolate dessert. She'd be programming her insulin pod to cover the spike her blood sugar was bound to have.

As she took care measuring out the coconut flour, her mind slowly settled. She had been unnerved from the moment Omar had slid the ring onto her finger. The three-pronged diamond sparkled every time the sunlight caught it. She could tell the ring was aged. Had it belonged to an older woman in his family? The thought had almost sent her running from the courtroom.

The ring was much different from what Ja— *he* had given her. The one she had given to her mother to hold on to. She should probably sell it now, considering she wore another man's ring on her finger. Trinity really wasn't sure why she'd held on to her old engagement ring, but with no job or prospects, the money could certainly come in handy. For now, she would focus on settling into this new life and pray for the tension to fade from her thoughts.

"Trinity'll be good for the girls."

Omar nodded, peering at his father-in-law. "I think so."

"Christine would be glad someone's caring for them." Rock turned his rheumy gaze toward him.

A lump appeared in Omar's throat. It was one of the things that had made him question the arrangement. "You think?"

"I sure do. Y'all meant the world to her. She wouldn't want ya wandering around lost and unhappy."

"Thanks, Rock." Omar appreciated his father-in-law's vote of confidence, but still, he wondered. Would Christine *truly* be happy with the circumstances?

"Anytime, son." Rock clasped a hand on Omar's shoulder. "Now I'ma mosey on out of here and let y'all celebrate."

Omar wanted to call him back. Instead, he watched as Rock shuffled out the front door. Giggles floated from the kitchen, begging him to join in on the festivities. But he needed to sit for a moment and reflect. For the second time in his life, he was married.

The hairs on the back of his neck raised. Would this marriage be like the first? He shook his head. Of course not. He didn't love Trinity like that. At most, he could pray that it would chase away the loneliness that had been his life the past two years with Christine gone.

Lord God. He paused, wondering what to say. What was he truly thinking? Feeling? He ran a hand down his clean-shaven face. He'd put a razor to his goatee this morning, thinking it would be appropriate. Some things one just did before a wedding—even a justice of the peace one.

Lord, please bless our union. Please rid me of this unease. No, it wasn't unease. More like discomfort. He'd teased Trinity about her anxiety, but he'd been trying to ignore his own thoughts of the morning's events. Not once had he imagined marrying anyone but Christine.

She'd been his high school sweetheart and willing to wait for him through his college dreams, and later his time at Bluebonnet's firefighter academy. The early years of their marriage had been fraught with infertility, until finally, they'd been blessed with Faith. Hence her name. They'd wanted to commemorate the blessing of their daughter.

They'd been so excited to learn they'd be parents a second time. But when she went to her first doctor's appointment when she was pregnant with Joy, they'd found out Christine had cancer. The doctors wanted to eradicate it quickly and aggressively. With one decision born of love, Christine had sealed her fate and blessed Joy with a future.

Lord God, please bless this union. Please rid both Trinity and me of this awkwardness. We've always been comfortable with each other. I pray it remains that way.

He didn't want to lose his best friend by trying to help her. Omar stood. The only way to have normalcy was to act like everything was just fine. Hopefully the forced feeling would fade and true ease would take place.

When he walked into the kitchen, the girls were sitting in their high chairs, licking chocolate-covered spoons.

"Daddy!" Faith squealed, jutting her spoon forward. "Choc'late."

"Is it yummy?"

"Mmm-hmm."

Both girls grinned in unison, diving for another dip of the batter.

Trinity held out a wooden spoon. "Want some?"

"Nah. I'll wait for the real deal."

She arched an eyebrow, flicking some braids

over her shoulders. "Omar Young, you're never too old to lick a cake-battered spoon."

A memory of them as children licking spoons at Trinity's parents' house came to mind. His stomach rumbled. "Is that your mama's recipe?"

"Nope." Her dimples flashed as her eyes twinkled with mischief. "But trust me, it's good."

"All right. Hand over the spoon and no one has to get hurt."

The girls giggled when he licked the spoon. He wiped at his mouth. "Are we having just cake for dinner?"

"'Course not." Trinity tapped her foot on the floor. Then she shrugged. "I hadn't planned that far out. How about spaghetti?"

"Should you be eating that?"

She arched an eyebrow at his question. "If you must know, I did bring zucchini noodles."

"For everyone?" He held his breath. He wasn't a huge vegetable fan.

"Just myself, Omar."

Phew. "Okay then, that sounds good." He turned toward Faith and Joy. "Girls?"

"Yes!" Joy squealed.

"She likes p'ghetti a lot, Miss T." Faith shook her head knowingly.

His three-year-old had a tad bit of a know-it-all personality, but Joy was happy to let Faith take the reins. He prayed they'd always get along so well.

"Great. Omar, wanna help?" Trinity motioned toward the kitchen area.

"Sure."

He hung his jacket on the back of a chair, rolling up his shirtsleeves. *This.* This was the normalcy he wanted. They had cooked together countless times before. Why should today be any different?

She's your wife now. It's bound to be a little different.

Maybe if he could respect that, his acceptance would minimize the effect of any changes in their relationship. He didn't want to lose their easy camaraderie. Working on autopilot, he grabbed a pot and filled it with water. At the same time, Trinity grabbed a skillet.

"Please tell me you have defrosted meat." She propped a hand on her hip and an arch lifted her brow.

"Uh…" He shrugged and opened the fridge. "No ground turkey or beef in here."

"What is in there?"

He turned to Trinity. "Chicken breast."

"Chicken Parmesan?"

"Sounds good to me."

Their movements were in sync as they each carried on their assignments in quiet. Omar couldn't help but compare it to how he interacted with Christine. She didn't like anyone in her space and had considered the kitchen hers alone. She'd always said that nothing brought her more joy than cooking for him.

But Trinity wasn't like that. She expected him to pitch in no matter what. Their friendship had always been that way. Apparently, a couple of *I do*s and wedding rings wouldn't change that. Which was a good thing, right?

Then why are you dwelling on it?

He gave a mental shrug. It was like signing the marriage certificate and knowing Trinity was his wife according to the state of Texas had set off all his thoughts and imploded his emotions. It was a good thing neither one of them expected romance or a happily-ever-after. That was more pressure than he could stand.

Right now, he just needed to focus on the here and now. Later, he'd have time to sort his feelings and confront the idea that he'd betrayed Christine today.

Chapter Five

"T, lots bubbles?"

Joy's wide black eyes reminded Trinity of a doll, so sweet and pure. "Sure, sweetie."

Trinity stuck a finger under the stream coming from the faucet to check the temperature. The water had taken a bit to warm up, but now it felt just right. She put the stopper in and grabbed the bubble bath bottle. The scent of chewing gum hit her as the liquid quickly foamed and bubbled up in the water.

"Yay!" Faith squealed as Joy clapped with glee.

They were so easy to please. Dinner had gone smoothly, at least that's what Omar had said. He believed the girls were on their best behavior for company's sake. The thought unnerved her. She remembered the disbelief her parents had expressed over her taking care of two toddlers.

So far so good, right?

Joy tugged on her shirt and pointed at the bubbles. Trinity scooped one up and pressed it to the little girl's nose. Her sweet giggles filled the bathroom. The two looked so much alike they could have been twins. The only difference between them was Faith had an inch or two more in height, which made sense because she was the oldest. Plus, her face and body held a roundness that made her a little more solid than Joy.

"While the tub fills up, let's go grab y'all some pajamas, 'kay?"

"'Kay," they chimed.

She held their hands as they walked down the hall and into their bedroom. The pink walls were picture free and without adornment except for the cursive *F* and *J* above their toddler beds. Pale pink wisps of curtains hung from the window between the two beds.

"Where's your dresser?"

"In closet." Joy stuck her thumb in her mouth.

"Oh, don't do that, sweetie." She gently tugged on Joy's thumb.

Trinity walked into the closet, marveling at the space. The space was bigger than the one in her old apartment, with plenty of room for the girls to grow into. She opened the top drawer and grimaced. It looked like a burglar had snuck in and rummaged through the contents. The other drawers were worse, but finally, she found a pair of pajamas for each girl.

"Aha!" She held them up.

Note to self: organize the dresser drawers. She didn't know if she should blame Omar or the girls for the complete disarray.

She turned to show Faith and Joy, but the room was empty. "Girls?" She spun around, checking the closet. *Nothing.*

Unease filled her. "Faith? Joy?" She called out into the hall. The sound of giggles lured her forward, and she darted into the bathroom.

Trinity sighed in relief as she took in their sweet faces from the doorway. But that relief quickly faded. Her body jerked, taking in the scene of mayhem before her. Streaks of pink liquid lined the floor, cabinets, and colored the sink and toilet. Joy's hands froze in a smeared pile of bubble bath on the floor. Judging by the pink handprints on the walls, she'd been doing her own version of finger painting.

Faith stopped midmovement, holding the bubble bath bottle upside down, allowing it to drip into the toilet. Trinity couldn't figure out where to fix her gaze next. So, she did the next best thing.

"Faith! Joy!"

The girls' eyes widened at the snappish edge to Trinity's scolding.

Faith's bottom lip began to tremble, and Joy's

little body shuddered with sniffles as her eyes filled with tears.

No, no, no!

Trinity squatted to their level, but it was too late. They let out their own variations of a piercing cry that echoed in the bathroom and probably made its way downstairs to where Omar was supposed to be relaxing and watching TV.

Her first mom duty and she'd failed. Footsteps pounded on the stairs, and Trinity winced. Would Omar get angry?

"What in the world?"

Trinity pivoted on her heel, peering up into Omar's flabbergasted expression. His mouth had dropped open and his hands were raised in surprised confusion.

"They found the bubble bath." Even she could hear the chagrined tone in her words.

"Obviously," he replied dryly. He picked up Joy and patted her on the back to calm her down.

Why hadn't she thought of that? Faith's luminous eyes looked at her father as if she wanted the same comfort. Trinity held out her arms, but Faith bypassed her and headed for Omar. She gulped, telling herself the ache in her chest was indigestion and not hurt. After all, it was only the first day. Not even a real *full* day.

Ugh.

She'd been Miss T all their lives. Being the

stepmom would take some time for all of them to get used to. Trinity stood, ignoring the weird ping in her chest. "I forgot to put the bubble bath back into the cabinet. Sorry."

Omar sighed, nodding quietly in acknowledgment of her apology. He swayed gently back and forth, murmuring softly to the girls as their wails receded, and sniffles and hiccups took their place.

Not knowing what else to do, she grabbed a towel to clean up the mess. She eyed the toilet warily. Would bubbles overflow if she flushed it? The thought of toilet-water bubbles spilling over the bowl had her germ radar alert pinging on high. Still, she couldn't just let them sit there. She pulled out her cell phone and did a search on bubble bath complications. After finding her answer, she filled her lungs with air and pressed down on the handle. She sighed as the water went down despite the bubbles popping up.

"Trinity, the tub!"

She gaped in horror. *How did I forget?* She quickly shut off the water. She'd have to do better than this. "No overflow." She glanced back at Omar, whose brow had furrowed and lips flattened.

"Yeah, but it's too high for them to sit in. They're a lot shorter when they're sitting in a tub."

"Oh." Did she know anything? "I'll let the stopper out and put it back in once it's lower."

"Okay. I can help with the girls."

Trinity wanted to object, but obviously she needed supervision for their first bath.

Once the girls were in the tub, she and Omar worked together silently. After tucking them in, Trinity grabbed the dirty towels from the bathroom and headed for the laundry area near the top of the stairs. A bifold door hid the full-size washer and dryer from view. She grabbed the washer detergent and paused. Would the sound from the machine keep the girls from sleeping? She turned to find Omar and bit back a scream, covering her mouth with her hand.

"Omar!" she squeaked.

He chuckled. "Sorry. I didn't mean to scare you."

"It's okay." The hairs on her arms rose from fright. She pressed a hand to her heart, waiting for it to slow down. "I wasn't expecting you to be right behind me." She pointed to the machine. "Will a running washer keep them awake?"

"I don't think so. I usually do a load in the morning before I head to work. Nancy would help by drying and folding the clothes for me." He tilted his head to the side. "You hungry? I think all that excitement gave me an appetite."

Not at all. The night hadn't gone the way she'd thought, but Trinity didn't want to decline Omar's offer. "Sure."

"Good, we can have cake and ice cream."

She'd forgotten all about the cake. Even the girls seemed to have forgotten in the mix of the bath-time trauma. She'd have to remember to give them a slice tomorrow. Trinity focused on her friend. "You have ice cream?" *Dumb question.* She'd never seen Omar eat cake without ice cream; plus, he'd just mentioned it.

"Always."

A loose laugh tickled free and released some tension. "What kind?"

"Mint chocolate chip, vanilla, chocolate and probably some other flavors."

"Why do you have so much?"

He paused at the bottom of the stairs and met her gaze. "I'm a growing boy." He winked.

She chuckled as his warm brown eyes lit up with amusement. She followed him into the kitchen. Omar had already grabbed two bowls and was slicing the chocolate cake. He put a sliver of cake into her bowl and slid it over to her.

At the sight, her stomach awoke. But what was she supposed to do with that tiny piece? Sniff it? "That's it?"

"Trinity, you're diabetic."

Ugh! From one micromanager to the next. "I can have more than this. I'm not even sure how you cut a slice so small."

He added a bigger portion. "Better?"

"Yes. And one scoop of ice cream please."

He frowned, so Trinity pulled out her personal diabetes manager. The small Blackberry-looking device would give her the insulin needed to allow her to enjoy the food. "I'm not jeopardizing my health. Promise."

"Fine."

He added a scoop to the blue plastic bowl. Earlier she'd realized all his plates and bowls were made of plastic. She guessed that came with parenthood. They felt so light compared to her own dishes and even the ones her mom used.

"Oh, I almost forgot. I got you this." He pulled a wrapped rectangle-shaped package from the drawer and placed it in front of her. "Happy wedding day."

Her stomach dropped and she eyed the package warily. Why would he have gotten her a gift? This wasn't a real marriage. "What is it?"

"Open it. I promise it won't bite."

She tore through the wrapper and smiled, part relief and part joy. It was a package of sugar-free, chocolate-covered almonds.

"They're your favorite, right?"

She nodded, a grin slipping easily onto her face. "Thanks, Omar."

"Anytime." He squeezed her hand.

She hesitated, then plunged forward with her thoughts. "I didn't get you anything."

"It's okay. Think of it as a welcome home gift."

"Okay." She could do that. As long as he didn't call it a wedding present. She wanted no part of that farce.

Omar raised his bowl. "Cheers."

Trinity chuckled, tapping hers against his.

He took a big scoop of the chocolate cake and then dove into the mint chocolate chip ice cream. *Yum.* A noise of appreciation must have slipped out because Trinity asked if it was good. "Very." He finished swallowing. "Are you going to tell me what the ingredients are?"

Her eyes crinkled at the corners. "No, sir. Just enjoy."

"I will."

Silence settled between them as they ate. His mind shifted to the bath-time disaster. Thankfully a little cake and ice cream made the incident seem like a distant memory. Although now, his brain brought up the horrified expression on Trinity's face when he had walked in. His shoulders shook as he tried to repress laughter.

"What's got you going?"

He shook his head, pressing a fist to his mouth, but it was no use. Guffaws fell as his body shook. "You...should...have...seen...your...face." He gasped out in between bouts of laughter, then mimed a horrified expression.

Trinity's mouth parted and then finally, she joined in, shaking her head. "I think I was in shock."

"For a moment I thought you were going to cry like the girls. I'm pretty sure I saw your bottom lip quivering." He snorted, shaking his head.

"I was tempted. I've *never* seen such a mess."

"Oh, you should have seen Nancy trying to scrub permanent marker from the kitchen table once." His laughter subsided as he thought of his mother-in-law. He startled when Trinity laid a hand on his.

"I'm sorry, Omar."

"Thanks." He swallowed around the ache that seemed to always linger. Would the blanket of grief ever lift?

And how selfish was he? He got to see his girls grow up, to laugh over their antics...while Christine and Nancy would never have the chance.

He stood, the kitchen bar stool scraping the floors with a cringe-inducing noise. "I think I'll head upstairs."

"Are you sure? We could watch some TV or stream something." Trinity watched him closely.

Didn't he owe it to Trinity to at least hang out with her on their wedding day? She was giving up her independence just to help him raise his kids. Hadn't he put companionship in the pros column? "You're right. We should watch a movie."

Trinity nodded and relief pushed back the worry in her eyes. "Action film?"

"You don't want to watch a chick flick?"

"Always. But I thought you preferred action movies."

"Of course I do, but I think you should pick." He almost said because it was their wedding day, but he didn't have the energy to try to normalize it anymore.

Don't focus on it.

Usually they'd flip a coin to pick a movie. *Of course.* Why hadn't he thought of that sooner? He pulled a quarter out his pocket. "Flip for it?"

Trinity smiled. "Perfect. I call heads."

He flipped it in the air and pointed to the back of the coin. "Tails." He rubbed his hands together. "I wonder what I'll choose."

Trinity rolled her eyes, but a small smile covered her lips. They moved into the living room, and he scrolled through the movie options. He didn't want to completely bore her, so he selected the latest superhero movie. It wasn't a chick flick, but it wouldn't have her falling asleep either.

As they settled onto the couch, a comfortable silence fell between them. Omar let out a slow exhale. Right now, at this moment, he could believe they'd be okay. Bath time had been full of drama, but they both came out smiling. *Together.*

He looked at his best friend. "Thanks for being my friend, Trinity."

"How could I not be? BFFs?" She held out a fist.

He tapped his against hers. "Forever." It was their tradition, one they'd created as children. He'd refused to repeat the acronym and after much compromise, settled on "forever" to cement the statement. Omar slid an arm around Trinity, giving her a side hug. "I'm so thankful for you."

She rested her head against his shoulder. "Even though I messed up bath time?"

His heart twisted at the insecurity in her voice. "I thought that was Faith and Joy?"

"But I left the bubbles out."

"And one day I'll leave something out too. That's parenting."

"No wonder you always look exhausted."

"Hey." He gently shook her.

She laughed, straightening up to curl her feet underneath her.

"You just wait. Come Wednesday, when I get back home, we'll see how pretty you look after kid duty."

"Are you trying to scare me?" There was a hint of sass in her voice.

There was a comfort in knowing every nuance. He thought back to her questions. "I'm leaving you home with a two-year-old and a three-year-old. You should be shaking in those…" He snuck a look at the feet peeking out from underneath her thigh. "Socks."

Her chin tipped up and a look of steel entered her eyes. "We'll be just fine. You'll see."

"Okay. Don't say I didn't warn you." No one had warned him. His mom just said congratulations and sent baby clothes every few months.

"Humph." She shifted on the couch cushion and made a shushing motion. "Start the movie, naysayer."

"That's Mr. Naysayer to you."

They both laughed as he pressed Play.

Lord, thank You for this easiness between us. It helps relieve the awkwardness of the whole arrangement. Because at the end of the movie, he'd go to his room and his wife—Omar shook his head—would go to hers. *Oh yeah, Lord, this is all very strange.*

Whoso findeth a wife findeth a good thing, and obtaineth favour of the Lord. The verse blazed through his mind like fireworks. How was he supposed to feel about that? Trinity wasn't Christine and could never take her place. But did that mean he couldn't live a happy life with his best friend? So what if their marriage wasn't conventional—it could still be a bright spot.

He hoped.

He shifted, trying to focus on the movie and

shove life's questions to the back corner of his mind. Except he couldn't ignore Trinity's presence. Couldn't ignore the gratitude that filled him knowing she was here and he was no longer alone.

Thank You for friends, Lord.

Chapter Six

Trinity stared up at the ceiling, blinking the sleep from her eyes. Her bed was so comfortable, and sleep beckoned once more, but today was her first full day as Mrs. Young and stepmom to Faith and Joy. She couldn't succumb to the comfort of her blanket and pillows.

Lord God, please let today go well.

She rolled to her side and then sat up, stretching her arms above her head. She needed to get dressed for the day. Thankfully, she'd showered the night before to give herself more time this morning to prepare breakfast. Hopefully everyone would appreciate her meal.

Grabbing her cell phone, she pulled up the app that monitored her blood sugar. A soft smile creased her face at her numbers. Within normal range. Only question was, should she fix a breakfast they could all eat or make one everyone assumed all diabetics ate? It would avoid judgment like Omar's with the cake last night. There was so much people didn't know about the disease. Having Type 1 was completely different from having Type 2. As long as she ate a relatively normal diet, just like everyone else, she was fine—well, with the help of her insulin.

The kitchen was quiet and empty when she walked in. Omar always drank coffee in the morning, so she'd count that as her first wifely duty. She walked toward the old-fashioned coffeemaker, shaking her head. Why couldn't he have some trendy kitchen appliance? She knew it wasn't his style but counting out scoops was a chore. She would need to find where she put her fancy pod appliance.

After assessing the refrigerator's contents, she laid out ingredients for French toast and bacon. Once the bread sat warming in the oven, she turned on the skillet. After she got the girls up, maybe she'd make a little fruit salad. She vaguely remembered seeing some strawberries and blueberries.

The sound of footsteps broke through her concentration, so she turned.

Omar appeared, holding Joy in his arms and Faith by his side. "Morning, Trin."

Her nerves frayed at the sight. "Good morning. I was going to get them up." Why couldn't things run as planned?

"No need." He offered her a smile as he sat them in their high chairs.

This time she was a little slow. Next time she'd wake the girls first before making breakfast.

"Whatcha cooking?" Omar stepped next to her, and she jolted.

She wasn't used to being around other people so early. "French toast and turkey bacon."

"Turkey bacon?"

"You won't notice a difference."

"Okay." He smiled.

"Have a seat and I'll bring it to you."

Thankfully she'd already programmed her insulin dosage so she could sit down right away with Omar and the girls. Trinity placed a plate in front of Omar and then walked back to get one each for the girls.

"This looks great, Trinity." Omar's lips quirked, bringing out the crinkles that framed his eyes.

"Thank you." She put a slice of toast on her plate and some bacon. A quick glance at her phone told her that her blood sugar numbers were still good. Trinity turned to Faith, gesturing to the cut-up bread on her plate. "Eat up. Aren't you hungry?"

Faith knew how to use a fork and Trinity had even remembered to grab the kids' utensils.

Faith poked at the syrup-covered bread with her plastic spork. "Yucky."

"Try it." Trinity did her best to offer a look of encouragement.

"No."

Trinity bit the inside of her cheek, slowly exhaling. "I promise you, it's good."

"Good." Joy chimed in, bits of food flying from her mouth.

Trinity calmly wiped off chunks of bread from her arm and met Faith's no-nonsense expression. "Joy likes it."

"Sticky."

"That's the syrup, sweetie."

Faith's brow furrowed and her head dipped down into a glower. "I don't like s'up."

Trinity's gaze flew to Omar's. His eyes widened as he chewed on a piece of bacon, then he shrugged. "Nancy always made their breakfasts."

"She never made French toast?"

"No, they usually had fruit, I think."

"She only fed them fruit?" Trinity tried hard to keep the look of confusion and any hint of judgment from her face, but it was so very hard. Normally her face told all of her secrets.

Omar tipped his shoulder up in question. "I'm pretty sure she kept to Christine's food routine."

"What do you mean?" Her heart thudded in her chest. "How did Christine feed Faith?" Faith had been one when Christine had passed. Hadn't that been a strictly liquid diet?

"Well, I mean, Christine had ideas of what a kid should eat once able. She wanted our kids to follow a certain diet. Nancy made sure to carry out her wishes."

"Which was what, exactly?" How could Trinity institute something she had no knowledge of?

"Pure food. Clean food." At her blank look he continued, setting his bacon down. "Think the food pyramid on steroids."

She raised her eyebrow, gesturing toward his bacon.

"Oh no, that was her thing. I'm a firefighter. I need bacon."

Trinity chuckled, releasing the tension that had her shoulders heading for her ears. "Do you want me to feed them fruit for breakfast?"

Omar took a moment before replying. "Yes. I'm sure there are some kids' cookbooks around here. I think Nancy left them in one of the cabinets." He grabbed a stack of French toast from the serving plate and drowned them in syrup.

Cookbooks. She'd have to look for those later. Right now, she needed Faith to eat. "Do you like bananas?" she asked Faith, spying some near the fridge.

"Yucky." She shook her head, frown still in place.

Trinity sighed and got up. One kid was apparently happy with her calorie-laden breakfast. The other would stick to the regime her grandmother had put in place. She rubbed her forehead. *It's not that bad. What kid doesn't need fruit?* But the thought didn't keep her from feeling inadequate.

Apples. Oranges. Strawberries. Pears. Apparently, fruit was a staple in the Young household.

She turned, asking Faith if she liked any of those things.

"No!" Faith hurled her spork across the room and wailed. "Mimi!"

At the heartbreaking cry for their deceased grandmother, Trinity rushed forward, but Omar picked Faith up by the time she made it to the table. He rubbed his daughter's back and rocked her in his arms. Trinity looked at Joy and noticed her lip began to tremble.

No, no, no.

Rushing to Joy, Trinity bent down, smiling at her. "Is your breakfast good?"

"Faith sad?" Her lip quivered, but the tears remained hidden.

"Yes."

"I sad?"

How was she supposed to answer that? "Do you want a hug?"

Joy nodded, flinging her arms upward. Trinity unhooked the high chair and lifted Joy into her arms. The little girl wrapped her chubby arms around Trinity's neck and sighed. "I not sad."

Trinity's heart turned over in her chest and a deep feeling of love swelled within. "I'm glad you're not sad. Do you want to finish your breakfast?"

Joy popped up, lifting her head from Trinity's chest. "I done."

Trinity glanced at her plate. Empty. *Huh.* "Want some banana?"

"Nanner!" Joy clapped, her chubby cheeks scrunched up with delight.

Trinity placed her back in the chair, locking the toddler in safely. She wouldn't make the mistake of leaving them unattended and able to roam free. Or to fall and injure themselves. Passing Omar, she asked if all was well with her eyes. He nodded yes as he strapped Faith back in.

While she cut Joy's banana into manageable pieces, Omar came up to her. He leaned against the counter, facing the girls.

"Sorry. Faith has always been picky at dinner. I guess I never noticed her moods at breakfast. Nancy usually ran the show."

How couldn't he know? It seemed like something a parent would realize. Then again, Omar had been oblivious to a lot of things since Christine's passing. Grief had aged her friend and worn him down.

She straightened her shoulders and squeezed his hand. "No worries. I'll figure out what she wants. Do you have to leave soon?" She wanted to congratulate herself on the neutral tone of her voice.

For reasons she couldn't explain, hurt had taken up residence in her heart when Omar informed her he'd be returning to work today. He hadn't wasted any time in going back to the station. Then again, they needed his paycheck to survive. He'd been off since Nancy had passed, so she really couldn't ask him to take more time off. She shoved her contradictory feelings aside.

"Yeah. My shift starts at noon. I'll be home tomorrow at the same time."

Trinity nodded. It would be interesting to see the effects of his schedule. She always knew the Bluebonnet Fire Department had twenty-four-hour shifts on and twenty-four hours off, but she'd never been the wife of a firefighter until now.

A wife. It sounded so strange, false even, since theirs wasn't a normal arrangement. Her mind flashed back to that day in white. And the missing groom.

"I also work Saturday." Omar broke through her thoughts. "So I won't get off until church is over."

"Will you be able to eat afterward?" The church always had a potluck after service.

"Yeah, I can leave the station and go straight there."

"Sounds good." She smiled, letting him know all was well. "Go finish your breakfast."

"All right." His eyes moved back and forth as he studied her. "Faith likes strawberries."

"So, she lied earlier?"

"I think she's just upset."

"But you didn't tell her not to lie."

"Trinity," he huffed, "she's three, and it's early."

Not too early to teach kids. Still, an inner sense cautioned her to bide her time. She'd be home with the girls all day. If Faith did something wrong, Trinity could tell her the importance of doing right. Surely little changes here and there would help them all adjust to the new arrangement.

She brought the bananas to Joy and then set a plate of strawberries in front of Faith. The three-year-old huffed, folding her arms across her chest and turning in the chair so her back was to Trinity.

At-ti-tude. She'd heard the term *threenager* from some of the church ladies who had younger kids. Now she knew what they meant. Instead of picking a fight, Trinity calmly ate and asked Joy and Omar questions here and there.

Slowly but surely, Faith began to eat the strawberries, sneaking a wary gaze at Trinity every now and again. She wanted to laugh at the suspicion in Faith's gaze, but she was just glad the little girl finally ate something. Hopefully it wouldn't take them a long time to get used to Trinity's presence as an all-day affair.

"Something you wanna share, Young?"

Omar looked over the refrigerator door at his colleague. "About what?"

Jeremy Rider leaned against the fire department's kitchen counter near the fridge. His arms were crossed, and his eyebrows were elevated as he stared at Omar skeptically.

"Seems you had a little fun without telling anyone." He smirked.

"What in the world are you talking about, Rider?" Omar straightened to his full height. The younger man always had something smart to say, and he wasn't in a mood for it.

There had been this odd tension between him and Trinity before he'd left for work. Having lunch seemed to alleviate some of it. Still, Trinity had seemed withdrawn, but he hadn't had time to find out why. Maybe the discord was making him extra prickly where Rider was concerned.

"That ring on your finger."

Heat flushed the back of his neck. "Oh."

"Oh?" Rider's voice went up an octave. "Just oh?"

"I got," Omar cleared his throat, "married."

"Wait one minute." Rider held up his hands and then turned his head toward the open bay. "Y'all get up here."

Great. Did he have to explain the circumstances of his marriage to the whole crew or could he just mention he married Trinity? They hadn't really discussed what to tell anyone outside of their family.

Footsteps pounded against the stairs until everyone—his captain included—filled the kitchen and dining area.

"What's all this racket, Rider?" The captain squared his hands on his hips, a look of irritation covering his dark brown face.

"Cap, get this. Young got married." Rider hooked a thumb Omar's way.

The captain's gaze swiveled to his. Omar resisted the desire to take a step back. It was like having your father glower at you after you'd done something without his permission. Not that he needed the captain's permission. But still, Cap looked angry.

"This true?"

"Yes, sir. Got married yesterday."

Low whistles and exclamations rent the air. "Yesterday?"

"Yes, sir. I figured you didn't want me to do that today."

The captain's lips flattened at Omar's quip. "Who did you marry, Young?"

He gulped. This is where it got tricky. "Trinity, sir."

The captain wiped a hand over his mouth, eyes bugging out. He shifted under the light, the rays hitting his bald head with a glare.

Omar adverted his eyes, only to see knowing glances and high fives passing between some of the crew. "What?" He held out his hands. "I'm not allowed to get married again?"

"My office, Young." The captain straightened and pivoted.

Omar glanced over his shoulder, shaking his head at Rider.

The firefighter gave a sheepish shrug of his shoulder. "I didn't realize he'd flip like that. Sorry, man." He clapped Omar on the shoulder and sauntered off.

Only an hour into shift and Rider was already causing trouble. Omar headed for the captain's office, wishing he could avoid the visit. As he jogged down the stairs, he sent up a quick prayer for help before double knocking on Captain Simms's door.

"Enter."

Omar walked in, shutting the door behind him. "You wanted to see me, sir?"

"Have a seat, Young."

He stifled a sigh and did as ordered. On a good day, Captain Simms was a friend. Today, it had yet to be determined.

The captain took his time stacking paperwork and straightening his desk before finally looking Omar in the face. Cap's black eyes were dull with fatigue. He interlaced his fingers, sliding them behind his head. "You married Trinity, huh?"

"I did."

"You don't love her." The captain rolled his eyes. "I'm sure you do the way a friend does, but not like a husband."

If he squirmed in his seat, would it release the tension coiling inside? "Is that a question?"

"Of course not. I deal in facts, as should you."

"Trinity knows where I stand."

"Does she?" The captain's low baritone was contemplative. "Is she home with the girls?"

"Yes."

"Will she be returning back to work in the fall?"

"She was laid off."

"Huh," the captain grunted, stroking his mustache. "Why don't you go on home."

Confusion filled him. "Today's not my off day."

"You just got married."

"It's not like we're on a honeymoon, Captain. Plus, I just used bereavement leave." Omar jerked back as Captain Simms squinted his eyes.

As if six feet two inches of corded muscle wasn't scary enough, Cap had a glower that could reduce the biggest of men into awkward adolescents trying to assert themselves in the face of authority. "I know for a fact you have more leave available."

Still, Omar tried to reason with the man. "There's no one to cover my shift."

"We'll manage."

"Captain—"

"In fact," a calculating gleam glittered in his eyes and dismay clenched Omar's stomach muscles, "I don't want to see you until next Tuesday."

A whole week! What was he supposed to do until then?

"I'd imagine hang out with your wife."

Omar's head jerked up as he realized he'd voiced his question out loud. "Right. Yes, sir."

"Dismissed. See you next Tuesday."

"Wait, sir." He slid his hands down his legs. "I need to get Trinity added to my insurance."

"Let me contact HR. I think you can log in to our intranet and do that."

Omar waited as the captain confirmed with the human resources department which website he needed to use to add Trinity to his benefits.

Cap slid him a sticky note with the pertinent information. "Luce says you have thirty days to add her, but to do it now rather than later."

"Yes, sir."

"'Bye, Young."

Omar left the office and stopped, standing there in the open bay, a little bit stunned by the turn of events.

Rider walked up to him. "What did he say?" He jerked his head toward the captain's office.

"He gave me the week off." *A whole week.*

"What?" Rider's jaw dropped and his eyes widened. "A vacation?"

"More like a honeymoon, Rider," the captain called out as he walked toward the back.

Heat crawled up Omar's face. It wasn't *like* that. He and Trinity had an understanding. Omar had no idea what game the captain was playing, but he'd figure out what to do with his time.

He swallowed. *Lord, I know the guys all have this idea of what our marriage is like, but You know better.* And just why was it so important that people continued to bring up their lack of romantic love? People had been marrying for convenience for years before "love matches" came around.

Still, it wasn't like he couldn't make the most of a forced vacation. He could try to see it as a blessing that would allow him to play with the girls and help Trinity transition to having two precious lives to watch over.

Understanding dawned. This wasn't some kind of punishment. This was a week off work to hang out with his favorite people.

Win-win.

By the time Omar walked through the front door of his home, he was convinced a week off would be a good thing. It would give him and Trinity time to get used to their new status and work out the weird kinks the *I do*s had brought. Maybe even pinpoint the source of the mysterious tension from earlier.

Except instead of finding calm and harmony, he walked into utter chaos. Joy's eyes were round circles as her head turned back and forth between Faith and Trinity. She looked like she was watching a ping-pong match.

He walked closer, trying to make out Faith's words through her tears.

"But I wanna be married."

Trinity tugged on the ends of her braids like she'd lost all patience. "Faith, sweetie, you can't marry your daddy. Plus, you're too young."

"I'm not two. I'm three." She thrust three fingers in Trinity's face and threw her head back, letting out a wail reminiscent of the last firework at Bluebonnet's New Year's Eve celebration.

Omar jiggled a finger in his ear and stepped forward. "What is going on?"

Trinity blinked. "Omar? What are you doing back?"

"I'll tell you later."

Faith ran to him, clinging tightly to his leg. He bent down, lifting her up into his arms. "What's wrong, sweetie?"

"Miss T says we no marry."

He looked at Trinity for further explanation.

"Faith asked me if she could marry you and when I told her no…" Trinity's voice trailed off as she gestured toward his daughter.

"Ah." How could he unravel this sticky situation?

"Sweetie, only mommies and daddies marry."

"Miss T is stepmommy, not real mommy."

He winced inwardly. Way to make things worse. He avoided looking at Trinity and instead carried Faith to the couch, sitting her on his knee. "It's kind of the same thing."

Faith folded her arms and glowered at him. "I wanna marry."

"When you grow up you can." He gave an inward shake of his head. No way he wanted to think—*worry*— about his daughters marrying.

As far as he was concerned, they wouldn't even be allowed to date until they graduated college.

"Fine." She pouted.

He kissed her forehead. "Is it nap time?"

"Yes." Trinity's whisper sounded like she was holding tears back.

"Come on, girls, let's go take a nap." Faith held his hand and Trinity picked Joy up and trudged behind him.

After changing them into new diapers and settling them down with some music, Omar closed their bedroom door.

Trinity leaned against the hall wall. "I am exhausted."

"You need a nap too?"

She shook her head. "I'm not sure if I had lunch."

He frowned. "Trin, you need to stop doing that."

"Yes, Dad," she said wryly.

"Sorry. Not to sound overbearing. You know I care."

She nodded. "You do." She straightened. "I'm sorry. Just a little short on manners right now." She tilted her head. "What are you doing back so early?"

"Oh, the captain gave me a week off as a congratulations."

Her mouth opened, then promptly shut.

"What?"

She shrugged.

"Come on, tell me."

"I just thought it strange you didn't even think to ask for some time off."

"I've been off for two weeks."

"And just got married." She pursed her lips. "Not that this is a real marriage, but still."

"You wanted me to stay?" Was that why she'd been tense this morning?

All this time, he'd been so focused on keeping their friendship normal, he never thought of the changes required of him simply because he was her husband now. Yes, he had to maintain his friendship with Trinity, but she needed him to lead them as well.

"I'm sorry, Trin. Forgive me?" He held out his arms.

"Yeah." She laid her head against his chest. "I'm not even sure why it bothered me so much."

"It's okay. This is new territory. We'll navigate it." And he'd remember to think more like a husband and still aim for that friendship balance. He hoped.

Chapter Seven

Was this week over yet?

Trinity slumped across her dresser, wishing for a few more minutes of quiet. Although Omar had been here to help her transition, life was hectic in the Young household. Turned out Faith, who used to love when Trinity came over, didn't like her constant presence now that they shared a house. And Joy, well, the two-year-old was a sympathetic crier. Absolutely draining on the emotions.

However, once the girls were asleep, Trinity's life took on a different tone. She and Omar had streamed a movie every night this week, sometimes watching them and other times using the movie as background noise while they talked about life. In those moments, she'd been able to unwind before the chaos began all over again.

"Trin-ty!"

She winced as Joy's high-pitched yell reached

her ears. With a sigh, Trinity slipped on her flats in a hurry while fastening the backs of her earrings on. She'd learned that getting dressed first was easier than starting with the girls. If she did it the other way, one of the toddlers was sure to be naked again by the time they needed to walk out the door to wherever they had to go.

Apparently, clothing was restrictive for them.

Joy stood in front of the bathroom door, wiggling in a universal dance.

"Just go in, sweetie."

"Can't," she whined, shifting back and forth.

Trinity frowned and twisted the knob. Locked.

"Faith, you in there?"

"No."

Trinity whirled around to see Faith standing in the doorway of her bedroom. Who was in the bathroom?

"What's going on?" Omar walked out of the master, looking at them all in the hallway.

Oh no. Had she somehow managed to leave the push lock in after her morning shower? She licked her lips. "Bathroom door's locked and Joy needs to use it."

His eyes widened.

Faith whimpered. "I sorry. I like button click." She looked at Omar. "Did I break it?" Her lip quivered, but Trinity didn't have time to comfort her.

She nodded pointedly to Omar. He dipped his head and kneeled before Faith to reassure her. Judging from the look on his face, he wasn't too thrilled with the situation either. "No, baby, you didn't break it."

"Trin-ty," Joy whimpered.

She scooped her up. "I'm going to run next door and let her use my parents' bathroom. You handle Faith."

Omar pulled his pocketknife out and squatted in front of the doorknob. "All right."

Never a dull moment. At least they could divide and conquer.

She hurried next door, all the while praying Joy didn't have an accident. "You okay?"

"No."

"We're almost there."

She pounded on the door of her childhood home. Sweet relief welcomed her when the door swung open. Her father stood there with an irritated expression that quickly softened at the sight of them.

"Joy needs to use the restroom, and ours is locked."

Trinity heard the sound of her father's laughter as she dashed to the half bathroom tucked behind the living room. She set Joy down in the nick of time. The little girl smiled sweetly at her, tears receding. After they washed their hands, they left the room at a much slower pace.

"See you at church," Trinity called out.

"Why don't you sit with us?" her mom asked, stepping out of the kitchen.

"I'll see what Omar says. I think he asked to sit with Rock this week. He's a little concerned." She bit her lip. Was that gossip or a common-sense statement?

"Rock's welcome to sit with us too. He shouldn't be alone."

"We'll watch over him, Mama."

"Or we could join y'all?" Her mother stared expectantly.

Uh.

"I just want to spend a little time with y'all, Trinity."

She nodded. "I'll talk to Omar. I need to go and finish getting the girls ready."

Pride shone in her mother's eyes. "Perhaps I can come over this week? Spend a little time with the girls?"

She nodded. Her mother had been itching for grandchildren for ages. Trinity knew her mom had been purposely holding herself back so that Trinity could find her footing. Guess the "honey-moon" was over. "Of course, Mama. I'll let you know when's a good day. See y'all at church."

"Later, baby girl," her dad called from the couch, listening intently to the sports channel.

She chuckled. If his team was playing this afternoon, he'd quietly exit the church's potluck to catch it. Probably grab a plate of food on the way out.

Trinity and Joy strolled across the grass toward Omar's house. She stopped, looking at the place. Maybe a good pressure washing would give the exterior a face-lift, help it not look so old.

"Whatcha lookin' at, Trin-ty?"

"The house."

"It sad."

"Is it?" She peered down at Joy, waiting to hear what the little one had to say.

"Mmm-hmm. Need fun."

"Oh really?" How could a house have fun? "What should we do?"

"Pway!" Joy threw her arms up, twirling in her nightgown.

Trinity laughed and scooped Joy up, tickling her. The sound of the screen door slapping shut grabbed her attention. Omar stood there, staring at them, his lips quirked into a half smile. Faith looked on hesitantly, like she wanted to join in on the fun but didn't want to let go of her anger. Trinity held out her hand, waiting for Faith to make a decision.

The little girl stared at Trinity's hand, then her

face, and back to her hand once more. Finally, her little legs pumped down the stairs and onto the grass. Trinity set Joy down and swung Faith into the air. This was the little girl she loved. The one who wanted to giggle and be swung around.

And that's what Trinity did.

She didn't stop until dizziness overtook her and let her know she couldn't play around forever. Carefully Trinity stopped and stared into Faith's eyes. "Was that fun?"

"Yes. Again?"

"We need to head for church now," Omar called out.

"How about later?" At Faith's nod, Trinity continued, "Let's go change really fast."

She neared the front porch and Omar held her gaze captive. She halted and cocked her head to the side, raising her eyebrows in question. Something lit in his dark eyes as he studied Trinity.

A strange little thump beat in her chest while her pulse pounded in her ears. "Did you need something?" The airy sound of her breath made her cheeks heat with embarrassment.

He blinked. Stepped back. "Uh, no. I'll wait out here."

"We'll be right back."

A little later, they each buckled a toddler into their respective car seats. Trinity gasped as she remembered her mom's request. "Oh, my mom wants to know if we'll sit with them."

"You know I wanted to sit by Rock."

"Of course I do. He's invited. Or they could sit with us?"

Omar rubbed his chin before closing the back door. Trinity followed and got in the front passenger side. "What do you think?"

"If Rock doesn't mind, sure. Whether it's in his row or your parents'."

"Great."

She settled back into the seat, looking out the windshield. "Is this going to be weird?"

"I don't see why it has to. No different than any other Sunday."

"True." Except now they had wedding rings on their fingers.

"It'll be fine."

She smiled briefly, thinking of how that had become the mantra of their friendship. If she could just tell her heart that and believe it, then maybe all really would be fine.

Trinity faced Omar. "What are we going to tell everyone?" She tapped her wedding ring. "Someone's bound to notice our new jewelry."

"Good question." He rubbed the back of his head. "I didn't really know what to say at the station, other than mind your own business."

She chuckled. "Yeah, that sounds a little rude,

not to mention that won't fly with some of the elders."

"How 'bout the truth. We're friends who wanted to be there for one another in good times and bad. Maybe even ask the pastor to make an announcement."

Trinity mulled over Omar's words. It was true, and they didn't have to add the details of her needing insurance and him wanting help with the girls. Because at the end of the day, that was a matter between husband and wife. Wasn't it?

"Okay. I think that's a good idea."

"All right. Then that's what we'll go with." Omar squeezed her hand before returning his to the wheel. "Besides, I doubt anyone will notice."

Everyone was staring.

Or at least that's how Omar felt. This Sunday was no different than any other Sunday, except for the fact they'd visited a justice of the peace and exchanged vows the week before. *But the congregation doesn't know that.* The whispers and pointed looks had to be a figment of his imagination.

When he walked the girls to their class, Leslie—the woman in charge of the two-and-three-year-old room—noticed his ring. Her eyes had gone wide and lips parted like a fish gasping for water. He quickly escaped and scanned the lobby for anyone familiar, friendly or at least someone who wouldn't ask a lot of questions.

He spotted Rock grabbing a cup of coffee at the hospitality table. "Morning, Rock."

"Hey there, Omar." Rock looked over his shoulder. "Where's your bride?"

The lady next to them popped her head up, spilling the sugar that had been balanced precariously on her spoon.

Uh-oh.

"She went to the restroom." Omar slipped a hand on Rock's shoulder, nudging him away from the table. "Do you want to sit with her parents this morning?"

"Oh no, son. You go 'head and get to know them better."

"Rock, I grew up right next door. The Davises know me."

"They know their daughter's *best friend.* It's different when said man becomes *the husband.*"

Was that true? Surely her parents wouldn't treat him differently. A strange unease slithered in his gut. "They invited you to join us, or we could all sit with you."

"Go sit with your other in-laws this morning." Rock clapped his back. "I'll be fine, Omar."

But would he? For some reason, the thought of joining them without Rock left Omar slightly unhinged.

Rock must have seen the look on his face because he peered straight into Omar's eyes. "You can do this."

"Just join us."

"How 'bout I come over for dinner tonight? That is, if it's okay with Miss Trinity." He gestured for Omar to turn.

Trinity stood near the restrooms, scanning the area for them. Omar raised his arm, motioning her over. A smile lit her whole face. Dimples winked with pleasure in her smooth brown skin. Her lips glistened from the maroon shade coloring them.

He blinked. *What in the world?* For a moment, he'd looked at Trinity like a man noticing a pretty woman for the first time. It had happened earlier as well. Standing on the front porch, she'd looked up at him, her brown eyes luminous. In an instant, he'd sunk into her gaze and a strange pull to move closer to her had him shifting forward.

Whoa. This is Trinity. Your best friend of twenty-something years.

That's right. Trinity Davis. *No, now she's Trinity Young.* He cleared his throat as she neared. "Do you mind if Rock joins us for dinner?"

"Not at all." She gave Rock a side hug. "How are you?"

"I'm hanging in there."

She nodded and straightened out of the church

hug. A whiff of flowers carried Omar's way. It was the same smell that lingered in the halls of his home. A smell that hadn't been there before Trinity moved in.

What in the world is wrong with me?

Since when did he notice how his best friend smelled? *Wife.* No, he'd had a wife. *Christine.* He loved Christine. Had been attracted to *only* Christine. Missed everything about Christine. *Christine.*

"Omar?"

He snapped out of it and found Rock and Trinity staring at him. Trinity's brow wrinkled, and her eyes held concern. Rock…well, there was a knowing look in his eyes that Omar didn't want to examine.

"Sorry. What did you say?"

"Trinity asked if we were ready to sit," Rock said. "I told her I'd be sitting by Bill today."

Omar was glad his father-in-law had a friend he could sit with. The two widowers had a lot in common. "Oh. Right. See you at the potluck?"

"I'll be there. You two?"

"We'll be there," Trinity answered. "I always help Mama out."

"Good." Rock leaned in toward Omar, whispering, "You got this, son."

Omar nodded and motioned for Trinity to lead the way. They entered the sanctuary to the strumming of music. Max was up onstage, playing on an acoustic guitar as the rest of the worship team got into position. Soon they'd invite everyone to stand. Little by little, people would make their way to the seats and stop talking.

Of course, most of the congregation had already quieted by the time Omar settled into a seat next to Trinity and her folks. He had a feeling they'd be the talk of the potluck with one or more inquiring minds wondering the status of their relationship, considering all the pointed looks at his ring finger. How had he ever been naive enough to believe no one would notice?

He was beginning to wonder if the explanation he and Trinity thought of would be good enough. A sense of trepidation trickled down his spine. Something had shifted in his mind. For once, Christine hadn't taken the forefront. Almost like he'd forgotten her. He bowed his head, guilt weighing him down.

Father, what have I done? How could I have forgotten how important Christine is to me? To our girls? Please forgive me for looking at another woman.

Omar shook his head. Trinity was his wife, which meant he hadn't done anything wrong, but boy, his mind thought differently.

Lord, what am I going to do? Recognition dawned and he straightened in his seat. *I don't have to do anything. It's all You. You're the answer to my problems, Lord. Please, please, take this...this awareness of Trinity away. Please help me maintain our friendship and honor Christine's memory. Amen.*

If others believed he had no obligation to his late wife since he was now a widower, then it was obvious those people had never lost a spouse. *'Til death do us part* didn't automatically sever ties. Death had parted him and Christine, but he still didn't feel released from those vows just yet. Only, now he'd said the words to Trinity.

If he wasn't able to let go of the vows he'd taken with Christine, how was he supposed to uphold them in this new union with Trinity? How was he supposed to love, honor and cherish Trinity in the here and now?

His head hurt about as much as his heart because death could break the vows again. What would he do if something happened to Trinity? He'd already lost one wife—would the Lord take a second one from him? The desire to retreat from life and go back to making it through one day at a time called to him. Sometimes feeling was worse than being numb.

Soon the music stopped, and Omar refocused his mind. The pastor could always pull him from his thoughts and into the Word. Scripture fed his soul and centered him. Unfortunately, the sermon didn't last and soon they were filing out of the sanctuary to head outside where the potluck would commence.

The acreage next to the church held white benches. Women and men placed slow cookers and other dishes on the long tables, buffet-style.

Omar glanced at his watch. He should get the girls and then come back. That way Trinity would have time to help her mom and he could get the kids situated. Omar walked over to Trinity, relaying his plan.

"Divide and conquer, right?" She grinned.

"Exactly."

She headed toward her mom and he turned, coming to an abrupt stop.

Jalissa Tucker stood, arms crossed and foot tapping impatiently.

"Afternoon, Jalissa."

"Omar."

He gulped. For some reason, Jalissa didn't like him. At least, he didn't think she did. She was never mean, but she didn't go out of her way to be cordial either. Since she was Trinity's other best friend, he always tried to smooth the waters.

"Hey, I'm on my way to get Faith and Joy. Did you need something?"

"Just wanted to know why neither one of you called and invited me to the festivities." Her mouth thinned as she tapped her left ring finger.

"Trinity didn't tell you?" That wasn't like her. He glanced over his shoulder, watching as Trinity carried a stack of paper plates to the beginning of the potluck line.

"Not. A. Word."

Yikes. "Are you sure?" He hedged. "Maybe you're missing a text or something?"

"Omar!" She stomped her foot. Her straight black hair swung with displeasure and her caramel skin reddened at the cheeks.

"I'm sorry." He held up his hands. "I had no idea Trinity hadn't said anything to you. We both talked to our parents, and I assumed she'd talk to you as well." He didn't know what else to say.

"Humph. Y'all walk into church together wearing wedding bands and getting the gossip mill up and running, and don't even let y'all friends know?"

He should have changed his Facebook status to "married." Maybe that would have been a better way to tell the whole world than to have all these awkward conversations. "Go talk to her. She'll explain everything."

Her light brown eyes squinted. "If you make her cry, I will…" Her brow furrowed as if searching for the appropriate punishment.

"Make me sorry?"

"You know I will."

"I wouldn't do anything to hurt her. She's my best friend."

"You mean *wife*."

"That too." Again, the desire to apologize to Christine for this whole fiasco weighed on him. He was supposed to help out a friend, not feel so convoluted over something he'd suggested with pure intentions.

"Go get your girls, Omar. Trinity and I have a lot to talk about."

He didn't need another invitation. With a dip of his head, he left. Maybe Jalissa would lose the attitude by the time he got back. Unfortunately, she wasn't the only one with questions. He got stopped numerous times, people staring pointedly at his hand, as if waiting for him to make some grand announcement.

He sighed. They should have asked the pastor to put their marital news in this morning's announcements. He just had to hang in there a little while longer. Then he could go home and navigate through the new normal.

Chapter Eight

Trinity curved her lips as high as they would go and prayed an innocent expression covered her face as Jalissa stopped before her with a hand to the hip and lips pressed tight.

"Uh-uh. Don't give me that look."

"What look? This is just my face." She resisted the urge to point to it. That was probably too obvious.

Jalissa took a step forward, her black hair shading part of her face. "You. Married. Omar?" Her eyes were wide and a note of hurt tinged her words.

"I did," she answered slowly, a hint of regret in her voice. She hadn't meant to hurt Jalissa. But how could Trinity admit she'd gotten married when just thinking about it made her reach for some itch cream?

"When?"

She shifted on her feet. "Monday."

"What!" Jalissa looked around and then lowered her voice. "And you're just now telling me? After you've been married almost a week?" A hint of distress flashed in her friend's light brown eyes.

Ugh. Trinity was a terrible friend. "I'm sorry for not telling you." And she was now. But Jalissa would have tried to talk Trinity out of it, even when she'd felt reassurance that it was the right move. Despite the fact that being married still unnerved her. Plus, Jalissa would have insisted on being at the ceremony and that would have been too much like a true wedding. If Trinity could avoid any similarities to before—when the church had been decorated to the hilt and she'd waited and waited—everything would be better for it.

"Why wouldn't you?"

"Just the mere thought gave me hives. Talking to you…" Trinity sighed. "It would have been that much more real." She shared her concerns about the justice of the peace being too much like before.

"Then it's not?" Jalissa dipped her head, looking at Trinity in confusion. "Y'all aren't in love? Haven't been secretly dating for months, or years?"

Trinity glanced around for prying ears, and

quickly shared the details behind her and Omar's arrangement.

"That's a little extreme, Trinity." Jalissa looked dumbfounded.

"Please, *please*, just be my friend." She puffed out some air.

"You're going to need one." Jalissa shifted her hair behind her. "But I'll be here. I already gave Omar *the talk*."

"The what?"

"You know. The if-you-make-her-cry kind of talk. We understand each other." Jalissa gave an abrupt nod, and Trinity chuckled inwardly.

Her friend was about a foot shorter than Omar and very petite. A stiff wind could knock her down…or at least have her leaning. To think Omar would be scared of her was comical. Then again, Jalissa did have a fierce temperament.

Trinity looped her arm through Jalissa's. "It'll be okay. I know what I'm getting into."

"Do you really?"

Not at all. She was beginning to feel off balance around Omar, like something stirred in the air to draw them closer. Trinity gave a mental shake of the head. That was ridiculous. They were the best of friends. This marriage was making her emotions yo-yo.

"Of course. We talked and prayed before going to the judge." Trinity patted Jalissa's hand in reassurance. "Everything will work out." She wished the words echoed in sincerity in her heart.

"I hope so."

Omar strode in their direction, Joy on his hip and Faith walking beside him holding his hand. Joy grinned when she spotted Trinity and held out her arms.

Trinity didn't think she could love the girls any more than she already had but being around them full-time had somehow made her heart grow ten times in affection. The love they gave so willingly, especially Joy, well, it was almost like she really was their mom—not merely a friend playing parent or the dreaded stepmother.

"Should we go through the line?" Omar asked. He eyed Jalissa warily and averted his gaze back to Trinity.

"Sounds good." She turned to Jalissa. "Would you like to join us?"

"No, but I *do* expect a phone call this evening."

"You can count on it."

Jalissa flashed a tight smile before squinting her eyes in Omar's direction. Trinity bit the inside of her cheek to keep from laughing. That girl was a hoot.

Omar met Trinity's gaze. "I saw the pastor on the way out here."

"Oh yeah?"

He nodded. "I asked him to make an announcement for us before the prayer."

Her stomach dipped. Soon everyone would know they were married. Ugh, why did her body have to flush with heat and bring on the urge to scratch? When would all things marriage-related not bother her so much? Jason was gone, hadn't looked back once, so why should she keep her head in the past?

"I hope that was okay."

"Of course. That was the plan." She tried to smile. "It'll probably lessen the stares." And the logical part of her brain could admit that. It was the not-so-rational part that wanted to run screaming the other way.

Change the subject.

Trinity kissed Joy's squishy cheek. "You hungry?"

"Mmm-hmm."

"Do you want some fruit?" She pointed to a fruit salad that gleamed in the sunlight.

Joy bobbed her head up and down.

After adding cheese, crackers and some deli meat to Joy's plate, Trinity led the little one to an empty picnic table. Omar followed with Faith trailing behind him. Trinity studied him, her pulse pounding strangely. Before they married, she could easily admit that he was handsome. Now the thought made her mouth dry and her heart perform strange acrobatics in her chest.

She needed to transform her mind and get it off of their new status quo. "I'm going back up to fix me a plate. Would you like me to make you one?" She gestured behind her.

Omar blinked and then a slow smile quirked the edges of his mouth. "That would be great."

Oh, my word. The way his full lips tilted in that half smile had her eyes focused on him with an intensity that made no sense. She swallowed, coming back to the present. "Okay. What would you like?"

He told her while cutting Faith's strawberries in half. The motion must have been second nature, but Trinity couldn't ignore the cuteness factor. There was something about a father and his children. After repeating his request to ensure she got it right, Trinity headed for the food tables, thankful for the opportunity to get a breather.

"Attention, everyone!"

Trinity turned from the table to where the pastor stood on a chair, hands cupped around his mouth. "I have a special announcement to make."

Her stomach rolled. *Here it goes.*

"This past week, two of our own got hitched."

Lord, please don't let me pass out. Because that would be ridiculous and maybe her marriage phobia was heading a little on that side of things.

"Please be sure to congratulate Omar Young and Trinity Davis, now Mrs. Young."

The *Mrs.* did her in. Her head swam as her knees wobbled. She really was married. In some *Twilight Zone* spin, she'd willingly said *I do.* Would this become a real marriage where she'd have to worry about her heart being trampled on? Could she fall in love and send Omar running the same direction as Jason?

Her breath shuddered. *No, no, no.* This was Omar. Her best friend, not the love of her life. Her desire to remain distant from love hadn't changed. Therefore, it wasn't even an option. It was all as simple as that.

People began clapping and some of the congregation members came up to her, giving her a hug and offering their congratulations. A weak smile struggled to appear on her face at the well wishes.

Trinity turned, quickly filling her and Omar's plates so she could go back to their table. The usual goodies were displayed, but there were also some new dishes. Every Sunday she tried to guess who made what. Sometimes the potluck contributors had been making the same dish for years and guessing was a matter of memory. Others, like the cheesecake beckoning to her, required more effort on her part. Wow, that looked delicious.

She pulled out her cell phone to check her blood sugar. Her numbers were a little high. Her lips pursed in frustration. No cheesecake or any other dessert for her. She grabbed a brownie and slid it onto Omar's plate. Thankfully she didn't have to stare at him enviously and watch him eat it. Brownies weren't her thing.

Omar gave her a smile of gratitude as she placed his plate in front of him. "Thank you."

"You're welcome. Did a lot of people stop by and say congrats?"

"Just the ones around us." He motioned to the nearby tables. "I imagine we'll get more congratulations when it's time to leave and everyone's done eating."

True. It wouldn't be so bad then, because escape would be near.

As if sensing the direction of her thoughts, Omar offered encouragement. "Don't worry, Trinity. We'll figure it out. *All* of it."

"You're right," she murmured. He usually was.

So why am I holding back tears? The whole affair had her so emotional. If she ever saw Jason again, she'd explain how much his simple no-show had altered her. Her self-esteem had plummeted, and her insecurities had increased.

Trinity took a bite of her food, all the while thinking of the conundrum of their convenient marriage. Sure, she would have health insurance and could continue to buy her insulin pods and other health care needs. Omar's fatigue had already begun to recede from his eyes and face. He looked rested and cracked more smiles than usual. Obviously, the arrangement had helped him. She'd even like to think the girls were a little happier. But had their marriage made a mockery of the institution?

Trinity had always believed marriage to be sacred. That's why Jason's abandonment hurt so much. Alone at the altar with no warning, she'd been unworthy the first go-around. What made her think agreeing with her best friend to exchange vows suddenly made her fit to be a wife?

Lord, please help me. My thoughts are twisting my insides up more than a funnel cake at a fair. Because even though she couldn't risk being in love a second time, Trinity didn't want to be found wanting as a wife either.

"Daddy, tell us a story," Faith pleaded as he hovered over her bed, prepared to tuck her in.

"What kind of story?"

"Pwincess," Joy shouted.

He chuckled and sat down on Faith's bed. "I'm not sure if I can tell a princess story."

"Try, Daddy." Faith poked out her bottom lip.

It must be innate in daughters to wrap their fathers around their little fingers. Trinity smirked at him as if she could see the war between giving in to his girls' pleading and escaping the art of storytelling. He'd always hated making up stories on the fly or anything to do with reading, while Trinity was the polar opposite.

"How about Trinity tell you a story?"

"No." Faith pouted.

"You," Joy encouraged.

Chuckling over his discomfort, Trinity sat on Joy's bed. "Yeah, Omar, tell them a story."

A week of tucking the girls in at night together, and he still had to do double takes when Trinity spoke or told the girls she loved them. He rubbed the back of his neck as he tried to think of a story. He must already know one, right?

It should be Christine telling them stories. He pushed the thought back and cleared his throat. "It was a dark and stormy night—"

"No, Daddy. *Once upon a time,*" Joy interrupted.

"Sorry, baby. Once upon a time, in a land far away, lived two young princesses in the kingdom of Young."

"Young? That's our name, Daddy." Faith's face scrunched up in irritation.

"Is it?" At her vigorous nod he continued. "Huh. Imagine that. Princess Faith and Princess Joy—"

"Us!" Joy's dark eyes shined bright with pleasure.

"Are you sure?" He cracked a smile to let her know he was teasing.

"Uh-huh."

"Well, did you know Princess Faith and Princess Joy had superpowers?"

"Princesses don't have superpowers, Daddy," Faith said with all the authority a three-year-old could muster.

"Why not?" Trinity asked.

"Superheroes have superpowers."

"Nuh-uh. Elsa powers!" Joy countered.

Omar suppressed a chuckle at the look of consternation on Faith's face. He continued his story. "Well, Princesses Faith and Joy were no ordinary princesses. You see, they could make others happy just by being kind. In fact, whenever someone was sad, they would visit the princesses to get better."

"Weal-ly?" Joy whispered.

"Really. They had the brightest, prettiest smiles that healed hearts."

"Okay. I like that," Faith said begrudgingly.

"I'm glad you do." He kissed her on her nose. "Okay, ladies. Time for bed."

"You didn't finish." Faith frowned.

"It's to be continued."

"What's that?" Joy asked.

"It means I'll finish tomorrow."

They groaned, and he bit back a laugh. "Love you."

"Love you, Daddy," they chorused.

"Love you, girls," Trinity added.

"Love you, Miss Trin-ty," the girls exclaimed.

He and Trinity headed for the door.

"Daddy, wait." Faith shot up in the bed.

"What's wrong?"

"You and Miss T say love you."

His eyes widened. Before June seventh, he would have easily said he loved Trinity. But putting a ring on her finger and wearing a different wedding band on his, suddenly made the formerly innocuous words feel completely different.

"We're not going to sleep yet," he said in a strangled voice. "We'll say it later."

"Okay." Appeased, Faith lay back down with a smile on her face.

He closed their bedroom door and leaned against it.

"Well, that was awkward." Trinity eyed him.

"Right?" He smiled in relief, thankful Trinity understood.

She folded her arms across her chest. "Actually, I thought *you* made it awkward."

"What? How?"

"Did you have to look so shocked by saying three little words?"

"We're not like that!" Why was she mad at him? She didn't even love him that way.

"*I* know that. *You* know that. The girls weren't even insinuating something romantic."

"It just caught me off guard since we're married now."

"That doesn't change anything, Omar. You know

that. We entered this for a mutually beneficial arrangement. Don't treat me like I have cooties."

"Trinity, come on. You mean to tell me it didn't surprise you?" He motioned for her to walk down the stairs.

"Of course not. I'm not falling in love again. *Ever.* And you…"

"I'm still in love with Christine."

"Exactly." She sighed, grabbing the end of one of her braids. "Sorry. I just don't want our friendship to change and it seems like it has anyway."

"You're right." He ran a hand down his face. "I overreacted."

"And I may have overreacted about your overreaction." Trinity tipped a shoulder up in a shrug.

He snorted. "Say that three times fast."

"No, thank you." Her lips quirked upward and the tension slowly eked out of the hallway.

"Still friends?" he asked, holding out his hand for a truce.

"Yes." She slid her hand in his. "Next time just say you love me. Remember, I already know it's as a friend."

But would Christine? She wasn't here anymore but telling his current wife he loved her felt like a betrayal to his late one. As much as he didn't want their friendship to change, for him, it already had.

Chapter Nine

Trinity looked around the living room, frowning. The functionality of the room was all wrong. Since she'd moved in, she'd constantly hit her knee on the end table while walking from the kitchen to the stairs, no matter that her brain knew it would be there. It became like a gravitational pull to her klutziness, setting her up for failure.

The clock showed about an hour before the girls would awaken from a nap. Since Omar was at work, she could rearrange the living room and surprise him. She nodded her head in decision and got to work.

Just as she shifted the end table into its new position, a voice called from the top of the stairs.

"Trin-ty."

She padded over to the stairs and looked up to see Joy behind the safety gate. "Hey, sweetie."

"I need bafroom."

Trinity jogged up the stairs, unlocking the gate and holding her hand out for Joy. "Let's go. Did you have a good nap?"

Joy nodded her head sleepily.

"Do you want a snack?"

"Uh-huh."

After they washed their hands, Trinity exited the bathroom with the two-year-old following closely. "Let's check on Faith first. Okay?"

"'Kay."

A quick peek showed Faith still sound asleep. Her thumb rested against her mouth and her lips moved up and down. Maybe she was hungry too. Trinity stood there, torn. An online support group for stepparents had warned her about waking a sleeping toddler. Yet, if she let Faith continue to sleep, wouldn't it mess with her sleep schedule later on? Or even throw off the snack schedule?

Schedules and structure were important for children. All the research pointed to that simple fact. But she also knew how demanding Faith could be when she'd gotten less sleep. *What to do, what to do?*

Making a decision, she walked into the girls' room and gently shook Faith. "Wake up, sweetie."

Faith whimpered in her sleep.

"Come on, Faith. Time for a snack." She

rubbed a finger down her cheek, hoping the motion would be a soothing way to wake her up.

"No," Faith drew out, rolling toward the wall and taking all the covers with her.

Trinity glanced behind her to make sure Joy still stood there and hadn't wandered off to some mischief. Relief relaxed her shoulders and she turned back to Faith.

"Fa-ith," Trinity sang out. "Do you want some ants on the log?" She resisted the urge to gag. She loved peanut butter, but it had no business touching celery or being dotted with raisins. *Disgusting.* "Faith, sweetie, wake up."

The little one jolted awake to a seated position, took one look at Trinity and let out a wail that would rival any opera singers'.

Trinity winced as she rubbed Faith's back. "It's okay. Time for a snack. You're okay."

"No snack. Nap!" She flopped backward, her body bouncing from the impact.

"But you like peanut butter and celery."

"Yuck!"

Ugh. Why, Lord? Why can't she just graciously accept the food like Joy? Why must she fight me every step of the way?

How had Nancy survived the tantrums? Worse, what if Faith only acted this way around Trinity? She was no longer the cool friend who came around to take them to the park or to storytime at the library. Obviously, Faith's joy at having a mommy had faded at the prospect of eating a snack Trinity suggested.

Her eyes widened with the epiphany. She had to beat the little one at her own game. "Faith, honey, what do you want for a snack?"

Faith stopped her thrashing, looking at Trinity warily. The little girl had a way of throwing looks at her that were GIF worthy.

"Peanut butter."

"Okay. Would you like it on crackers?" The combination frustrated the little one. Faith would cry every time the chewed-up food stuck to the roof of her mouth. And no amount of juice box drinking would dislodge it. They'd already had more than one instance requiring Trinity to scrape the food from its spot. Who knew parents were constantly assaulted with their kids' bodily fluids?

"No crackers." Faith glared, her nose scrunched with irritation. "Cel-ry."

Bingo. "Okay, let's go."

Faith ignored Trinity's outstretched hand and climbed out of the toddler bed. Trinity headed for the door, thanking God for the avoidance of a mega tantrum. Joy slid her hand in Trinity's while Faith opted for the railing as they descended the stairs.

They made it to the first-floor landing when her cell phone chimed.

"Hold on, girls. Let me see who this is." She pointed to the couch. "Have a seat."

"You moved them!" Faith placed her hands on her hips and stomped her feet.

Great. Apparently three-year-olds had opinions on furniture placement.

Trinity tapped on the message icon and clicked on Omar's name.

I got skunked. Can you make me a solution?

Trinity read the list of ingredients included in the text.

Why not use tomato juice?

According to my research, it won't rid you of the smell, just mask it.

She hoped he was right. No way she wanted Omar in the house if he smelled putrid. She shuddered, imagining an overpowering skunk smell.

What do you need me to do?

There should be a cleaning bucket under the sink. You can fill it with the solution and then set it out on the deck. I'm walking home and will be there soon.

Alright.

Trinity slid her phone into her back jean pocket and headed for the kitchen.

As she passed by the couch in its new place, Faith squinted her eyes. "Change it back."

"Not right now, Faith."

She fisted her hands. "Yes, now."

Oh boy. One thing at a time. Focus on Omar first, then you can handle the threenager.

Once she set the container outside, Trinity corralled the girls into their high chairs. "Joy, do you want kiwi?"

"Yay." Joy clapped her hands.

Well, at least one toddler was easy to please. She wondered if Joy would get a dose of attitude once she hit three. *Oh, Lord, please no.*

Shivers racked her frame. *Don't think about that right now. Just get through this moment.*

Trinity placed a spread of kiwi and cubed cheese in front of Joy and a plate of ants on the log in front of Faith.

"Thank you."

She stopped in surprise. "You're welcome, Faith."

The little one grinned, her head bopping back and forth. The clacking of beads from the end of her braids danced in the air. Nothing like food to soothe a hangry toddler.

Her phone chimed.

I'm here. Thanks for the solution.

You're welcome. Do you want lunch?

Could I get a tuna sandwich?

Sure.

Thanks. I'm going to the front since it's closer to the bathroom. Hopefully I'll smell better. I'll be down after a shower...or two.

She grinned. Tuna coming right up.

The front door opened and shut, and she heard footsteps pounding up the stairs. Trinity sat down to eat with the girls. Normally she'd wait until Omar walked in, but she'd already given herself a dose of insulin.

They all ate in silence until Omar's voice rang through the house. "What in the world, Trinity?"

She swallowed a piece of apple too fast and winced as it slowly slid its way down. She grabbed a cup of water and chugged a gulp down to help the food's passage. Taking a big breath, she made her way into the living room.

Omar stood there, a hand on his hip and a look of irritation covering his features.

"What's wrong?" She sniffed the air. A faint trace of skunk smell lingered in the air, but nothing horribly repugnant.

"You changed the furniture?" He gestured around the living room, a disturbed expression furrowing his brow.

"Yes. I kept bumping into the table. Besides, this way is more functional. It gives us more space."

His face shuttered. "But that's not how Christine had it."

Her heart dropped to gut level at Omar's whispered words. How had she never noticed it'd been the same way for years? What should she do? Say?

"When we came back from our honeymoon, we arranged everything just so until Christine proclaimed it perfect."

Oh man. An ache filled her throat. "Omar…" She cleared her throat, trying to get around the lump lodged there. How had she not noticed the depth of hurt he'd been going through? "I'm so sorry. I only wanted to help."

"What else do you plan on changing?" Hurt darkened his eyes. "Are you going to start redecorating the whole house? Throw out pictures?"

"What? No." Trinity shook her head, shocked. How could he think she'd erase Christine from his life? Omar had never spoken to her in such a tone. Hurt pierced her. "I really was just trying to help," she whispered.

"Yeah, please don't."

"Omar…"

His breath stuttered, his shoulders sagging as he turned away.

Her body wavered, rocking on her heels as the urge to go to him rose. He was hurting. *Grieving.* Something she had no experience with. But she couldn't stand here and let her friend think he was alone. Only she didn't know exactly what to do.

A cool hand touched Omar's forearm, and another found its way to the center of his back. He briefly noted the fresh flower smell that trailed in Trinity's presence.

"I am *so* sorry."

Her voice softened the ache permeating his heart. He wanted to give in to the utter shock of the changes in his home, but the note of concern in Trinity's voice cautioned him. Pulled him from tumbling into the pit of grief. *Barely.*

"I'll put everything back just the way it was if you want." Trinity's hand made small soothing circles on his back.

The motion reminded him of how he put the girls to sleep when they were babies. Joy had always needed the comforting touch until about two months ago. Faith, well, she always said she was fine but never complained if he rubbed her back until she fell asleep.

Only he wasn't a child.

"Why don't you sit at the table with the girls. I'll change it back while you spend some time with them."

Vaguely, he realized Trinity had said the same thing once before. Only now the words sank in the recesses of his mind. "You'd do that?"

He stared at her, amazed. His friend. *Best* friend. She'd always been one to help if someone needed assistance. Why did her offer of changing the living room shock him?

"Yes. If that's how you want the room to be, that's how it'll be."

Omar opened his mouth to give an emphatic yes but froze. The passage of time constantly had him grasping for remains of Christine's memory. The need to preserve all that she'd been to him weighed on him. Except he couldn't let his grief leave no room for Trinity to have a home. This house was no longer *just* his. Hadn't he promised to be a good husband to her?

"No." He pushed out a breath. "I'll get used to it." He turned toward her, pausing at the sorrow etched onto her features. Had he been too harsh? "Aw, Trinity, I'm sorry."

Her eyes widened. "Why are you apologizing?"

"The way I reacted. I shouldn't have... I mean,

I should have taken more care with my words." Taking a chance, he lightly slid his palms against hers and gently held on to her hands. "This is your home too. If you want to change things to feel more comfortable, you can. I don't want you to feel like you can't." He squeezed her hands, hoping she'd forgive him.

Her face flushed and she dipped her head.

Wait. Did she just blush? Before he could contemplate the thought any further, she looked up and stared straight into his eyes. His breath caught in his chest. How had he never noticed just how stunning Trinity truly was? The way her long lashes framed her dark brown eyes, letting her goodness shine from within…

His best friend was beautiful.

No, his *wife* was beautiful.

He stared at her, wondering why his heart felt lighter, held more peace. There was something about Trinity that just soothed every ache within.

"Daddy!"

Omar jumped backward, swinging around to look toward the kitchen.

"I'll go get them." Trinity rushed into the eat-in kitchen to get the girls.

He rubbed a hand down his face. *What was that?*

There had been some kind of moment between them. One look from those soulful eyes, and it was like a tethered cord tied them together. And even now, his heart thumped in his ears. He could feel heat climb up his neck.

He couldn't be interested in Trinity, couldn't risk letting his heart connect with another woman on a romantic level. What if he lost her like he lost Christine?

His gaze roamed around the living room, trying to find something to anchor him and his wayward thoughts. His stomach twisted as he spotted the picture of him and Christine on their wedding day. The frame was always perched on one of the end tables. Trinity hadn't removed the picture.

Although the table was no longer in the same place, she'd left a reminder of his late wife. He groaned and flopped onto the couch.

Lord God, what was that? A fluke? A side effect of close proximity? Please help me hold on to Christine and the memories and life we built together. Please keep my heart safe from going down that same path.

He didn't want to overcome his grief just to forget Christine and what they'd had or been to each other. Or worse, "move on" like some well-meaning friends liked to mention. He didn't want to fall in love again. Couldn't risk that all-consuming pain again. Omar gulped, running a hand over his face. He needed to talk to someone. *Anyone.*

Yet for the past two years, he'd stuck mostly to

himself. Besides Trinity and Rock, there weren't that many people he confided in. And he'd always been careful of what he told Rock. Always remembered that the man had lost a daughter. He never wanted his grief to affect Rock's.

No, there had to be someone else he could talk to who could keep the circumstances of his marriage quiet but offer good advice. Before he could recall his list of friends, the girls flew into the room. Faith climbed onto his lap with Joy quickly following suit.

He was like their personal jungle gym.

"You smell funny, Daddy," Faith said solemnly.

Joy giggled and covered her nose.

He gave himself a good whiff and sighed. "I got skunked."

Joy's eyes widened. "What?"

"Daddy got sprayed by a skunk."

"Go take a bath. With bubbles!" Faith clapped her hands.

Trinity smiled, shaking her head over Faith's. She was probably still horrified by their bathtime mischief.

"Maybe I will." The shower obviously hadn't worked. Then again, who wanted to sit in the filth of skunk spray?

"You should." Trinity stepped forward. "I'm going to take the girls to the park so they can get some fresh air."

"All right."

Then maybe he could figure out who to talk to. Might even call his parents. No, that wouldn't work. He didn't want his parents forming opinions that could negatively impact his friendship with Trinity.

"Have fun, girls." He squeezed them, kissing each on the forehead before he got up and headed upstairs.

Chapter Ten

The peace and quiet surrounded Trinity like a warm blanket. She stared out into the night from her spot on the porch swing. The girls had run her into the ground at the park today. They couldn't decide which activity they wanted to do, so they kept switching. *Often.* From the swing to the slide to the seesaw and back again. She'd been more than exhausted when they finally returned home.

Omar had seemed subdued all throughout dinner, barely cracking a smile. She couldn't help but blame the moment they'd had in the living room. The one where their eyes had seemed to lock and meld. What did you call that?

She could still recall the intensity of his gaze and the way her pulse had picked up pace as if running a marathon. It had been exhilarating and terrifying all in one. If she viewed it under a romantic lens, their friendship would be forever altered. It was weird enough being married to her best friend. To bring in romance, break the safety net she'd purposely put in place…well, it just didn't strike her smart meter.

She was thankful the girls had cried "Daddy." The cheer had been shouted from the proverbial rooftop and severed the moment. As life returned to normal, Trinity had made a note to remember falling in love was *not* the choice for her.

She took a sip from her glass of water and sighed, settling into the swing. The creak of the front door caught her attention and she peeked over her shoulder. *Omar.* "Hey."

Omar smiled and sat in the seat next to her. "Enjoying the quiet?"

"Mmm. I am." She took a deep inhale. "Seems like you finally got rid of the *eau de skunk*."

He chuckled and warmth slid into her middle. Omar had the best sounding laugh ever. It was like a warm Texas summer night. *Don't think of him like that!* Hadn't she just given herself a stern talking-to? Her heart couldn't stand any more trauma as it still hadn't fully recovered from Hurricane Jason.

"It'll be a while before I see one without flinching."

Right, the skunk. She shifted in her chair to get a better look at him. "How did you even cross paths?"

"We had to get a car out of a ditch today, because a drunk driver had lost control. Fortunately, he was okay, but his car…" Omar shook his head. "Anyway, I went down to hook his car up to the truck and there was the skunk. Like he was waiting for me. I took one step and poof." His hands made an exploding motion.

"Oh wow. Guess it'd be too obvious to tell you to stay out of ditches?"

"Hardy har har. He probably told his buddies to be on the lookout."

"Ew." She wrinkled her nose. "Make sure you tell them I had no part in it, so be kind to me."

"Ha. If I have to stink, you should. Married people share everything." The smile on his face froze.

Oh, Omar. Her heart hurt for him. He had no idea how to handle their marriage. *Lord, please help me know what to say. I don't want to make it worse.* "Omar."

"Hmm?"

"You know we're friends, right?"

"Of course I do." His head jerked in confusion.

"And no matter what, we'll always be friends." Oh, how she prayed it would be so. She reached out and squeezed his hand in comfort. "Just because I have your last name and live in your home doesn't mean I expect you to treat me like Christine."

"You're my wife."

"Technically." Surprisingly, the fact pricked like a splinter under her skin. She hadn't felt so contrary about it when they first opted to get married. It was like, all of a sudden, she wanted to matter—the way a wife would. *No. You're friends first and last. Romantic love never ends well. You were jilted, and Omar lost his wife.* Thinking of marriage as happily ever after was a liability she couldn't afford.

"But still my wife."

She stifled a sigh. "I know and you know, but it's not like we've ever kissed or even thought of each other in a romantic way.'" She couldn't. *Wouldn't.* "I'm *not* Christine. You aren't in love with me, and I'm not in love with you. I'm not the mother of your kids." Her voice softened as her mind struggled with these truths. Each one brought a hurt, but the why of it escaped her.

"Trinity." His brow furrowed and his tone held a slight note of scolding.

"What? It's the truth."

He reached for her hand, holding it loosely while staring down at their intertwined fingers. "Our marriage isn't like my first, but that doesn't mean I don't care about you."

"I know you do. I'm just trying to let you know, I don't expect a real marriage." But maybe, just maybe, she should.

She shook her head, attempting to shake the

thought free. Preservation was key and something she needed to remember, to brand in her mind so she wouldn't fall for trouble again.

"I don't want to hurt you, Trinity." His eyes pierced her. "I'd never want that. *Ever.*"

She bit the inside of her lip to keep it from trembling and gathered courage instead. "You won't. I knew what I was getting into." *Not really.* Did a person ever really know?

They could guess, speculate and dream up dozens of scenarios of how something would turn out. But life didn't always align with plans or intentions. If it did, then her heart wouldn't be feeling fresh pangs of hurt. Marriage to Omar was supposed to prevent that.

A man's heart deviseth his way: but the Lord directeth his steps.

Her mind understood that, but her heart wanted to try anyway. She couldn't map out her life, but man, she really wanted to. *Lord, please help me seek Your will and walk accordingly.*

"Still." Omar's voice brought her to the present.

"No." She leaned forward. "I'll be okay. You're grieving and that affects how you view everything. I know that. Remember, BFFs."

She held out a fist waiting for him to touch his to hers.

"Forever," he replied with a fist bump.

Trinity smiled and settled back into her seat.

She took another sip of her water. Hopefully it would calm her nerves and slow her racing heart. Despite her promise she'd be okay, Trinity was very much aware that could possibly turn out to be a lie.

Not an intentional one, but one caused by an unforeseen change of heart. *No, you're sticking to your plan. No romance. Plus, Omar's not going to fall in love again and neither are you.* Time to change the subject. "My mom is coming over tomorrow."

"Oh yeah?"

She took another swig. "I think she'd like the role of grandmother." She looked at Omar to see how he would handle the news.

"I can see that. She's great with kids."

"Is that okay with you?"

"Of course. Kids can't have too much family."

"You don't think so?"

"Not at all."

Huh. "Did you want a big family growing up?" She stared, curious. How had they never talked about this?

"I did. Being an only child was odd to me. It was one of the reasons I was glad you lived next door." He paused and smirked at her. "Once I got over the fact you were a girl."

She chuckled. "You just liked my tire swing."

"Sure did. Still do."

An idea came to her mind. "Want to go swing?"

"Really?" His lips twitched.

"Yeah. My parents might be up, but as long as we don't make a ruckus they'll never know." She held up the baby monitor. "Plus, we have this."

"Let's do it, then."

Trinity placed her cup on the porch and raced next door to her parents' house. She laughed at the sound of footfalls behind her. Ducking her head, she put forth all her speed and—missed. Omar grabbed the rope and sank into the tire. Laughing, she placed her hands on her knees to catch her breath as he rocked back and forth.

"Slowpoke."

"Your legs are longer," she gasped.

He quirked an eyebrow. "Excuses."

Trinity held the rope and stopped his movement. "It's supposed to be ladies first."

"Fine, fine." He rose and bowed. "After you, m'lady."

She turned away, settling into the tire, hoping Omar didn't notice the flush that had surely filled her cheeks. Why did she feel so strange around him all of a sudden? It was like a switch had been turned on, alerting her to his masculine charm. *No.* She needed to turn the thing back off and just relax. Remember the friend of her childhood and ignore the firefighter physique stretching his T-shirt.

She let the swinging motion of the tire calm her and fill her with peace. She tilted her head back and looked into Omar's smiling face, dancing in her vision. "Is it your turn?"

"Sure."

He stopped the swing and they switched places. Trinity pushed him, using a little more force to move him. He had the muscles needed to haul the equipment he was responsible for on duty. And it showed.

"Trinity?"

"Hmm?" She pushed him.

"Why did you let Jason turn you into a recluse?"

Her brain shorted. What to say? Did she tell him the belief she was unworthy of love? Or use the old-adage defense mechanism?

"I mean," Omar continued, "you're wonderful. You have a lot to offer. It seems a shame you never got back out there again."

Tears smarted. If she spoke, the tears might make an appearance, embarrassing her and cracking open the old hurt. Hopefully, Omar would take her silence as reflection.

"Just goes to show us men aren't very smart." Omar interrupted her musings.

"Why do you say that?" she croaked. She cleared her throat and repeated the question.

"Someone should have ignored your back-off

sign and pursued you." He stopped the swing and stood. "Showered you with the love you deserve."

She opened her mouth to argue and froze when he placed his finger on her lips. Tingles of awareness shot across every nerve ending. Why couldn't she stop noticing her best friend was a man?

"Your eyes flash fire sometimes," he murmured. "I just can't figure out what emotion triggers it."

Attraction. She wanted to deny it, but it was there like the pesky mosquitoes that stung her. "I'm not sure I know what you mean. After all, I can't see my eyes," she quipped, ignoring the tension in the air.

"Are you angry?"

She shook her head.

"Irritated?"

At herself? Yes. A thousand times. She'd already told herself the dangers of letting her emotions get involved. Omar needed to remain in the best friend box and stay there.

Then he leaned forward to whisper into her ear, instead of waiting for her response. "I'll just have to work on making you happy, so you won't mind a marriage of convenience."

Goose bumps covered the back of her neck.

"Your turn." He motioned with his hand toward the tire swing.

She moved, wordless, hating the tangle of her emotions.

* * *

The atmosphere had shifted once again. Omar couldn't explain what the change was, just that he had the innate desire to bring a smile to Trinity's face. How had he so easily slipped from wrecked confusion over Christine to wanting Trinity to be happy?

Then again, were those emotions mutually exclusive? He'd always wanted Trinity to be happy. She was his best friend, would always be his best friend.

Trinity pumped her legs, moving the tire swing. The cicadas continued to serenade them as he pushed her, so she didn't have to work so hard. Her fragrance floated on the summer breeze, and it seemed that nature itself was conspiring against him to set a mood for romance.

Protect your heart. If he could remember Christine, remember the pain that smothered him at her loss, then maybe he'd make it through this marriage intact.

"Maybe we should go back in. In case one of the girls needs us."

Trinity stopped. "Of course." She bit her lip, avoiding his gaze. "That would be best."

They walked side by side toward the house. He stuffed his hands into his shorts' pockets to keep from doing anything stupid, like reach out and hold her hand. Although he'd often held her hand to make a point in the past, now there seemed to be a romantic overtone attached to it. *Or it's all in my head.*

The urge to break the silence tugged at him, but what could he say? They'd already hashed out the awkwardness on the front porch earlier. To claim something was different now would be a mistake. Maybe he should just keep quiet until he could look at Trinity as the friend she was, forget June seventh and the vows that tied them together.

Before Trinity could open the front door, he laid a hand on her elbow to stop her. "Hold up."

"What's wrong?" A look of confusion covered her face.

"I…" *You what?* "Never mind." He dropped his hand.

"You okay?"

No. I'm stuck in my feelings. If Rider could get a peek at his thoughts, he'd clown Omar. He sighed, running a hand down his face. "I guess I have a lot on my mind."

"More than earlier?"

He gave a noncommittal noise. "I'll work it out."

"You sure?"

"Yeah." Because he had no choice. If he didn't, he'd become a bear to be around. He just needed a moment to gather his thoughts.

"Okay, then I'm headed for bed."

"Night."

"Night, Omar."

He watched as Trinity walked inside and headed for the stairs. Omar closed the front door softly and leaned against it. Earlier, he had tried to call a church friend for advice but ended the call before Zeke's voice mail could pick up. Maybe he should give him another ring. Omar pulled his cell phone out of his back pocket and found his friend's number in his contact list.

"Hey, Omar. What's up? That's twice in one day you've called."

"Yeah, sorry I didn't leave a message earlier."

"Everything okay?"

Omar moved toward the kitchen. He didn't want to sit in the living room. Not with a picture of Christine there as if watching his inner turmoil. He also didn't want to have to whisper. The kitchen would give him a little more privacy.

"It's about Trinity."

"You mean that little announcement you made at church?"

His face burned. "Yes, that."

"Why did you do it?"

He sighed and glanced toward the doorway. "Because it was mutually beneficial. She gets health insurance, and I get help with the kids."

"Wow. I don't even know what to say."

That would *not* work. He needed help. "I prayed about it."

"And…"

And what? Sometimes he didn't trust the response. Not for any fault on the Lord's. Never that. But he didn't trust himself. How much was he projecting in a prayer, and how much was he *not* listening? Sometimes, he got in the seasons of listing his needs without taking the time to be still and hear. He never knew if he should keep praying or when to believe he received an answer.

Omar rubbed his forehead. "I thought it was the right thing to do. The girls are laughing more than ever."

"And you? How are you adjusting?"

"I'm conflicted."

"Before we go any further, let's pray."

Omar bowed his head as Zeke prayed. He thanked the Lord for bringing Zeke to mind, who was currently working on a theology degree at night. During the day, Zeke made cold calls for the sales department he worked in, and on the weekend, he worked the sound booth at church.

"Okay." Zeke cleared his throat. "What's going on?"

"I…" Omar glanced at the doorway one more time then lowered his voice just in case. "I think I'm starting to have feelings for Trinity."

"What do you mean? Like *feelings*, feelings?"

He cleared his throat. "Yes. Being around her brings me a peace I haven't felt in a long time. And suddenly I'm concerned about her happiness." He shook his head. "I'm not saying this right. I've always cared about her happiness, but now *I* want to be the one who makes her happy."

His heart stopped. *No, no, no.* He couldn't walk down the love path again.

"Has that ever happened before? I mean before y'all married?"

"Never." Then again, there was that one summer. "Wait."

"You thought of something?"

"Yeah. The summer we turned sixteen. I had a little crush on her."

"Why didn't you act on it?"

"She was my best friend and I didn't want to ruin that. Then Christine moved here that fall and the rest was history."

"What's preventing you from acting on it now?"

"What if I fall in love with her and she dies? Diabetes has fatal complications. I can't lose another wife, Zeke. Losing Christine crushed me. There are days I can function and others where the reminder of grief hits me anew. Not to mention the guilt of feeling like I'm forgetting Christine."

"That's a lot, man. Let's take it one by one.

Trinity's been a diabetic for a long time. I'm not saying it would happen, but how do you think you'd handle it if y'all were just friends and she passed away?"

"Badly. But honestly, I've always expected her to live to an old age. Only now that I've said *I do*, it's like my brain is intent on reminding me what happens when your heart gets entangled in the love-'til-death. It's a whole different level." And he couldn't risk going through that depth of heartache again.

"That is true." Zeke paused. "God doesn't want us to live in fear, Omar."

"I know that in my head." He closed his eyes, gripping the cell.

"Then continue seeking God every day until your heart catches up."

And wasn't that what he was afraid of? But Zeke was trying, so the least Omar could do was thank him. "Appreciate you taking the time for me, man."

"Anytime. I'll be praying for you."

"Thanks." Omar hung up and stared at the phone, unsure of what to do next.

Chapter Eleven

"Hey, Mama." Trinity moved aside so her mother could cross the threshold.

Her mom kissed her cheek. "How are you, sweetie?" She pulled back, peering up into Trinity's eyes.

Sometimes their height difference seemed stark, and other times Trinity forgot she was taller. "I'm good." *And confused.*

Last night's swing excursion had left her feeling a little discombobulated. Only she couldn't confess that to her mother who was probably already worried about Trinity's marriage. She hadn't forgotten the disbelief her mother voiced when the subject first came up. Trinity closed the door and motioned for her mother to make herself comfortable.

"Where are those precious girls?" Her mom

clapped her hands together, a look of glee brightening her face.

Trinity grinned. "Eating a snack."

Her mother walked alongside her as they headed for the kitchen.

"Aw," her mom murmured.

Joy happily munched on her food as Faith daintily ate each morsel, folding her hands in her lap while chewing.

"Hey, girls, say hi to my mama."

Joy waved, bits of banana flinging in the air with the exuberant movement.

"Miz Davis your mama?" Faith's eyebrows shot up, making her dark eyes appear bigger.

"Of course she is. Don't you remember going to her house to play on the swing?" Trinity sat down at the same time her mom did.

Faith vigorously nodded her head. "Then your mama our grandma?"

"Uh…" She threw a panicked look at her mom. Omar knew how her mother felt about the girls, but Trinity hadn't actually asked what the girls should call her. She'd been too busy working through the scenes of the tire swing last night.

A hint of something special had filled the night air as they'd taken turns swinging. It was almost like they'd stood on the precipice of something bigger. But that was silly to think, right? Besides, she had plummeted to earth long ago. Jason had shattered her heart beyond repair. Surely no one wanted the mere pieces that remained. And even if they did, she couldn't risk her heart turning into confetti of heartbreak.

"I would love to be your grandma." Her mom leaned forward, a huge smile on her face.

Trinity pulled out of her thoughts and took in Faith's beaming face and her mom's joy. At least she could give her heart to these girls.

"Trin-ty?"

"Yes, Joy?" She grabbed a wet wipe and began cleaning her stepdaughter's hands.

"You my mama?" Joy pointed to her chest, her big brown eyes staring up at her.

Trinity's breath hitched. Why hadn't she and Omar discussed all the potential changes marriage would bring and what those would mean to the girls? It was one thing to cross a bridge when one came to it, quite another to be alone and having to test the rickety wood herself. Should she say yes and tell them to call her...what exactly?

Lord God, please give me some wisdom here.

Her mother squeezed her hand underneath the table.

She could go with the basics. "Well, see, since I'm married to your daddy, that makes me your stepmom. Remember?"

"What's step?" Faith asked.

Oh boy. Trinity wanted to say it meant technically she wasn't their mom, but how did one explain that to a two-and three-year-old?

"It means," her mother interjected, "that Trinity will always be here for you and will be your parent like your daddy."

Mom to the rescue. She wanted to hug her in gratitude.

"Can we call you Mommy?" Faith asked.

Yes, please. She would love that. "Would you like to?" Her voice came out calm despite the mental cartwheels she was doing. *Wait.* Would Omar flip out? He hadn't handled the rearranged furniture well. What would he think about this? He had to know she would never want to replace Christine.

Joy nodded and Faith paused, a look of concentration on her face. Finally, she gave a shrug of the shoulder. But something told Trinity Faith wasn't as blasé as she portrayed.

"How about we ask your daddy what he thinks when he comes home. Okay?"

"'Kay," the girls chimed.

Phew. Crisis averted.

Although she'd still have to broach the subject with Omar. The idea made her grimace inwardly. That impending conversation was sure to be difficult. But at least she'd ensured he wouldn't come home to hear the girls calling her Mommy or some other variation.

Good thing he's on shift.

Fortunately, the rest of the day went by without any further deep conversations or disasters. As she stared up at the ceiling that night, Trinity couldn't help but replay Joy's request for her to be their mom.

Lord, I want that. I want them to feel like they're blessed to have me because they've undoubtedly enriched my life. I want to see them grow into wonderful young ladies, and eventually fall in love.

Hopefully their love stories would be better than hers—jilted at the altar and now a bride in name only. She didn't want that for Faith and Joy, but was there even such a thing as true love? Trinity shook her head. Obviously, there was. Her parents were nearing forty years of marriage. Not to mention the forever kind of love Omar had had with Christine.

And a teeny, tiny part of her wanted that. *Enough already. You do not want to be in love! Remember standing at the altar all alone? Everyone staring at you with pitying expressions?*

It had been beyond mortifying. Her heart had shattered in full view of family and friends, and not to mention the guests that sat on Jason's side of the church, wondering where he was. His mother had been horrified but no more so than Trinity. Thankfully her parents and Omar had been there to shelter her from the fallout. Her mama had sent the guests on their way while Jalissa had wiped away her tears.

Dealing with the caterers and the other businesses that had a hand in making her day perfect had been an extra nightmare. But compared to how big a hit her self-esteem had taken, paying a wedding baker for a cake she didn't eat had been nothing.

Thankfully, Omar had been there for her— would *always* be there for her. That didn't mean she needed to be foolish and fall in love with her best friend. She shook her head. No, the best thing to do would be to remain his friend and be the best stepmom to his girls. She had to be there for Omar this time.

If only she could see how the impending "mommy" conversation would go tomorrow. Maybe if she made Omar a big lunch. A full stomach would help the discussion waters be placid versus a class five rapid. All she would need to do was figure out how to broach the subject.

Lord, I pray You'll guide me in the conversation and soften Omar's heart. Please help him be honest if he's not ready for me to be their mom in name. She bit her lip, trying to decide if she had any other requests. *Lord, I would also like Your help with my emotions. I feel like a seesaw going back and forth between attraction and dread. If I could just settle on one...* Not that she wanted to dread love. More like she needed to be okay if it didn't happen.

Like she was before they'd had midnight swing rides and deep stares.

Omar opened the front door and took in a whiff of what smelled like barbecue chicken and French fries. Trinity walked out of the kitchen and into the living room, greeting him with a smile.

"Hey, Trin." Omar moved to sit down on the couch, rotating his neck to work out the kinks. He'd slept wrong on his neck during his shift.

"Hey, there. I made you some lunch." She gestured back toward the kitchen. "That is, if you want to eat right now."

Trinity always made sure he had something to eat when he came home. He appreciated that more than he could say. "Yes, that sounds good." He offered a smile and what looked like relief flashed in her eyes.

Was she nervous about something? Before he could ask, Trinity asked him about his shift as they took their seats at the kitchen table.

"It was quiet."

"That's a good thing, right?"

He made a *meh* motion with his head. "It makes for a slow night." He never wanted a fire, but sometimes the empty hours loomed before him. Gave him too much time to think.

"And that's bad?"

"Not bad, just boring." But he didn't want to focus on himself. "What about you and the girls? Did you have a boring time?" He grinned, already knowing the answer.

"Well, actually," she paused, "the girls asked if they could call me Mommy."

His head jerked up. "What?"

The world froze as Trinity's words penetrated his terror-induced brain fog.

She licked her lips in a nervous fashion. "The girls asked yesterday when my mom was over. It started off with them wondering if she was their grandma now. Then they wanted to know about moms and what a stepmom was. Our conversation just naturally ended up there." She shrugged as if it was simply matter-of-fact.

Maybe to her it had been. But his kids calling her *Mommy* was so much more.

He stared down at his plate, trying to choke down the bite that had turned to ash in his mouth. His emotions were so overwhelming, he wasn't exactly sure how to sort them out. He wanted the girls to have a motherly influence. It was one of the positives of this marriage of convenience. But would Christine fade from their life in the process?

Omar dragged in a breath and focused his gaze on Trinity. "I see."

"And…is that okay? Are *you* okay?" She cracked her knuckles, all the while biting her lip as she studied him.

He honestly didn't know. The logical side of his brain thought it made perfect sense and he was happy the girls felt close enough to Trinity to want that type of relationship. And the other half kept saying *What about Christine?*

"I'm not sure what to say, Trin." His voice was low as he struggled to keep his tone even, devoid of emotion.

Her brow creased. "Look, I know this is a tough conversation. I've been praying about it since they brought it up, and I told the girls I'd talk to you about it first."

"I appreciate that." However, his tone contradicted his words a little bit.

He was floored. Didn't all his past conversations about their mom matter? He'd shared pictures of how beautiful Christine was with each pregnancy. Told the girls how much she loved them. Did none of that hold weight?

Trinity reached out and squeezed his hand. "Omar, it's okay for you to say no. I don't mind being Miss T or simply Trinity to them. It's who I've always been, and it *is* my name."

He gave a half smile at her attempted joke, then

drew in a breath to bolster himself. "And part of marrying me was getting a family of your own." Which meant he had to figure out how to adjust to the change, to live in the present.

But wow does it hurt, Lord.

"Yes, but nothing has to change at your expense. I don't want them calling me Mommy if it's going to bring the Oscar or Eeyore out in you."

A real laugh fell from his lips. "Already watching too many kids shows, huh?"

"Oh, believe me. I can reference them and sing their theme songs as well."

"Hey, some of them are catchy."

She shook her head. "Ear worms."

"I want to say yes." He rubbed a hand down his face.

"But?"

"I feel raw right now."

"Understandable." She withdrew her hand, a sympathetic smile on her face. "Maybe we should just eat and change the subject for now."

But he couldn't. Trinity had dropped a major bomb, and he wanted to retreat and think about it. Pick apart the details and nuances to examine it under his mental microscope.

"Trin-ty!"

The sound of Joy calling for her warmed his heart. If she had said Mommy would it have ached or been bittersweet? He watched his wife walk out of the room to get his daughter.

His wife. He gulped. If he thought of her only as his best friend, would that keep his heart from becoming entangled? Keep it safe in case the worst ever happened?

Lord God, what do I do? My mind's a jumble of thoughts. The girls calling Trinity Mommy. Me thinking of her as my wife.

What he really needed to focus on right now was the *mommy* situation.

Can I really deny my daughters the chance to call someone Mom? To forge that relationship and let it guide them through the years?

Their arrangement to marry and Trinity's desire to protect herself from hurt again meant she'd never have children of her own *to* call her Mommy. Was it fair to rob the rest of Trinity's life of the pleasure of having kids and all that came with them, including the honorary title?

Wow. When he thought about all the ramifications, it seemed selfish to say no. If he'd been divorced, that would have been a different conversation. Being a widower came with the tricky balance of honoring his late wife and making room for the new one.

Only he didn't want his acceptance to remove Christine's place in the girls' life. She'd always put their family first, and now thanks to a seal from the state of Texas, Trinity was in that circle. Which meant she was family and the girls' new mom.

He sighed. *Okay, Lord, I get it.* He needed to graciously accept the changes. *Please help me do that.* Because right now, he didn't feel the strength to do so.

"Daddy!"

Joy jumped into his arms, and he kissed her chubby cheek. "How's my girl?"

"Good."

"How come you're up?"

"Not sweepy."

"She went down at eleven thirty." Trinity's voice came from behind him.

An hour and a half wasn't bad for a nap. "Do you want to go to the water park?" He looked over Joy's head to peek at Trinity, who nodded in agreement as she ate her lunch.

"Yay." Joy placed her hands on his face. "Daddy happy?"

He'd get there. "Is Joy?" He gently placed his forehead against hers.

"Yes. Mommy?" She pointed to Trinity.

His heart pounded in his chest. "Yes, Trinity's your mommy." His voice trailed off in a choked whisper as he struggled to keep his eyes from leaking his emotions.

Joy grinned and wiggled, trying to get out

of his arms. He placed her down and she scampered right to Trinity, raising her arms in the air. He watched as Trinity scooped her up, and Joy placed her hands on Trinity's cheeks.

"Mommy."

Trinity's eyes watered.

He'd made the right decision. Trinity deserved a family and with the way she'd been guarding her heart, well, a marriage of convenience had opened a door for her dreams. Now he felt the need to protect his feelings.

Chapter Twelve

Trinity's nerves rattled as Omar pulled into a parking spot. Tension had radiated from him ever since she dropped the mommy bomb. He didn't cringe when Joy called her *Mommy*, but he hadn't been cheering either.

She looked over her shoulder toward the girls, sitting in the back seat. They practically vibrated with excitement in their car seats. At least someone was happy.

Don't let it get to you.

But the hurt coursing through her spoke of the pain lancing her heart. She didn't know why she wanted Omar's approval so much. Well, not approval but consent. Which he'd given, albeit grudgingly. Intellectually, she knew he wouldn't be happy about the girls calling her Mommy, but she hadn't wanted him to be so shocked either. Perhaps it was a deeper sign of his grief.

Once he put the vehicle in Park, Trinity hopped out of the Jeep to unbuckle Joy. Omar had already unhooked Faith and grabbed the diaper bag in the process. He'd probably get the stroller before she managed to free Joy from the car seat. Why was the tab so difficult to push?

"You got her?"

"I'm good."

Omar came to her side of the car. "You sure?"

"Yes." It came out more jubilant as the seat belt unhooked. She smiled, took Joy out of the car and swung her into the double stroller. "You girls ready?"

"Yes." They beamed at her.

Children were such a precious gift from God. *Thank You for letting me be in their lives.* She straightened to find Omar staring at her. "What?" She looked down, searching for anything out of place.

"Just thinking. Nothing's wrong." He gave her a closemouthed smile.

That look often appeared when something bothered him. Trinity wished she could see his eyes to really gauge his mood, but he wore shades to block out the Texas sunshine and her prying eyes. Come to think of it, she had on a pair herself, so no one would be peering into anyone's eyes.

Not that Omar would. They weren't like that.

His grief over Christine wouldn't allow for anything more. He'd straight up told her there would never be anyone else. And that was fine.

Just fine.

She didn't want to be in a relationship. They only brought heartache and despair. Plus, she couldn't compete with longing for a deceased spouse. She would come up short every single time. She'd had enough of being found wanting.

"Trinity?"

"Hmm?" She glanced up.

"The passes are in the diaper bag."

"Oh, right." Her cheeks heated as she dug through the front pocket. When had they stopped at the ticket counter? She must have been walking on autopilot. The water park employee smiled, taking the passes from Trinity. After he scanned them, she tucked them back into the bag.

She looked at Omar. "Did you pack sunscreen?"

"No. I don't even know if we own any."

"Let's stop over there." She pointed at the nearby gift shop. The prices would be outrageous but at least they'd all be protected. She'd found out the hard way that her brown skin could sunburn. She'd hate for the girls to experience that form of torture.

After applying some on Faith and Joy, Trinity switched to her own shoulders before offering the bottle to Omar. Her eyes scanned the family crowds at the water park. A lot of moms were wrestling with their children alone. Yet some of them had their husbands with them, representing the American version of a family unit. The same look she and Omar displayed. But they were merely presenting a facade.

She sighed. Since when did the arrangement bother her so much?

"I think we should head to the waterworks area." Omar's words broke through her contemplations. "The girls can walk through the water sprays."

"Sounds good."

The water park wasn't that busy today. Thursday was their full-price day for non–pass holders. Perhaps that's what kept the crowds from being overwhelming. Then again, maybe most people were working while their kids were off at summer camp somewhere. Either way, it was nice to have the place relatively quiet.

They picked a shaded table to sit under, and Trinity placed their bags on the bench seating as Omar unbuckled the girls. She sat down to watch as Joy and Faith ran toward the sprinklers. Their beaded braids clicked with their movement as they shouted with excitement.

A woman parked her stroller at the table situated to the right of Trinity. She snuck a peek at the little boy in the stroller. He grinned a gap-toothed smile her way while holding on to a stuffed puppy and gnawing on the ear.

"He's so cute," Trinity said to the stranger.

"Thank you. Are those your girls?" She pointed toward Faith and Joy.

Trinity's cheeks flushed and she resisted the urge to peek at Omar. Instead, she cleared her throat. "Yes, our girls, Faith and Joy."

"Oh, I just love those names." The woman rubbed her swollen belly. "I'm having a girl this time around and have been trying to figure out names." She pointed to a redheaded boy playing in the sprinklers. "I'm excited since I already have two boys."

"Congratulations. What are their names?"

"This little guy is Hunter, and the one splashing with your girls is Gunter."

"Cute. And you're braving the water park alone?"

"Oh no." She gave a sheepish smile. "My husband went to get a locker for our other things. I overpack every time."

Trinity chuckled. The compulsion to pack for every possible emergency was real. Omar had packed the diaper bag to keep Trinity from being "overly anxious" as he put it.

"I'm Beth." The lady stuck her hand out, leaning over the stroller.

"Trinity, and this is Omar." She placed a hand on Omar's shoulder. He shifted his gaze from the girls and greeted Beth.

"Y'all are such an adorable family."

Omar dipped his head in acknowledgment. "I think it's the girls that bring the cuteness factor."

Beth chuckled. "Kids garner us adults attention we wouldn't get otherwise."

"So true." Just the other day an older woman had stopped Trinity to chat with the girls, remarking at how cute they were.

Omar stood and smiled. "I think I'll play with the girls."

Trinity nodded and turned to find Beth watching them. "How long have y'all been married?"

"Um, we're actually newly married. And those are my stepdaughters." She was pleased she kept herself from fidgeting. She'd even said the *M* word without the desire to scratch at imaginary hives.

"Oh." Beth placed a hand over her heart. "That just hits me in all the feels. Did y'all have a whirlwind romance?"

Trinity almost choked on her spit at the question. She drew in a ragged breath, trying to school her features and find a look of calm.

"Mommy!" Faith shrieked.

Trinity whirled around and stared as Faith flailed about, swinging her arms around. *Oh no.*

Omar tried to grab Faith to calm her down, but she rushed straight into Trinity's arms.

"What's wrong, sweetie?"

"Bee. Bee. Bee!"

Trinity grabbed Faith's arms and held them to her sides. "Look at me. Take a deep breath for me."

"Did it sting her?" Omar asked.

"Hold on." Her eyes never left Faith's, hoping to reassure the girl she was okay.

Fear covered the sweet one's face and her eyes darted around as if searching for the offender. "Where is he?"

Trinity glanced around. "I don't see him, but if he comes back, I need you to be calm. Can you do that for me, brave girl?"

Faith nodded, beaded braids swinging with the movement.

"Did it sting you?"

"She got stung?" Omar asked.

Trinity shushed him. "Did it touch your skin? Land on you?"

"N-n-no. Scared me."

Trinity let out a breath and wrapped Faith in her arms. "You're okay, sweetie."

Faith's little arms squeezed Trinity's neck, but she didn't mind. There was comfort in knowing she could soothe another's ache even if she couldn't figure out how to care for her own.

* * *

Today was the firehouse's family day. Every year the captain rented some bouncy houses, hired a face painter, and brought in entertainment in the form of a clown or some other kids' performer. When Christine had passed, Omar had always felt awkward coming to the event with just his girls. Like he'd worn a sign saying *widower*, which sent all the other firefighter wives into a state of pitying glances and *oh dears*. Now that he was remarried and Trinity was coming, all he could think of was the comment made by the woman from the water park: *Y'all are such an adorable family.*

Giving the girls a family had been one of the pros of getting married and he could tell how much they'd begun to thrive under Trinity's care. It confirmed the rightness of their decision, but now his heart had begun to want a life that would only bring heartache. He couldn't let this marriage become real to him. Maintaining some sort of distance would prevent his heart from falling a second time—because unlike jumping out of a burning building, there was no inflatable device for one's heart to land on.

"Young, your family just walked in."

Omar spun around at Rider's announcement. "Thanks. I'll go meet them."

"Everything okay? You're looking a little peaked."

He shook his head. "Don't worry about it. I'll live." And that was the problem. He'd lived and Christine hadn't. Cancer was cruel and no respecter of persons. He couldn't guarantee that Trinity wouldn't suffer a similar fate and once again, he'd be on his own.

And every cliché about life not being fair blared in his head like a doomsday alarm.

But he had to shake it off. Trinity and the girls were here now and would expect him to be happy and ready to participate in the fun.

Omar wiped a hand down his face and followed Rider through the bay and outside. Some of the firefighters' wives had set up tables—buffet-style—with potluck offerings. The bouncy houses were full of little ones and their giggles punctuated the sounds of adult conversation.

He spotted Trinity talking to the captain's wife. She wore a long red dress that showed a hint of her sandals. Her braids cascaded behind her shoulders. And even from this distance, he could see the sparkle of her wedding ring.

His gut clenched as he stared down at his own. Had saying *I do* cracked the barrier around his heart? Allowed him to see her as more than just a friend? *Get it together, Young.* He drew in a breath, ignoring the ache in his chest and strolled over to say hi.

"Hey, Omar." Trinity grinned, shading her eyes with a hand.

She looked pretty and he couldn't deny he was happy to see her. "Hi, there." He nodded to the captain's wife. "Mrs. Simms."

"Omar." She offered a smile. "I wanted to congratulate you two."

"Thank you." They spoke simultaneously.

He looked at Trinity. "Where are your sunglasses?"

She shrugged. "Misplaced them."

"One of the girls probably found them. You want me to see if I have an extra pair?"

"That's all right. I'll be okay."

"Y'all are so sweet," Mrs. Simms exclaimed. "I love watching newlyweds when the bloom of true love is fresh and new."

Omar tensed. He didn't want to be in love. Didn't want that hurt again. Granted, he couldn't tell Mrs. Simms that.

"I think what you're seeing is years of friendship, Mrs. Simms," Trinity said. She sent a quick smile his way. It reminded him of the conversation they'd had about loving one another. They were the best of friends. If only he could keep his mind focused on a friendship level of feelings instead of wondering *what if.*

"I almost forgot y'all've been friends forever."

He smiled. "Mrs. Simms, if you'll excuse us, we're gonna go get the girls."

"Certainly."

He motioned for Trinity to follow him.

"How's your shift going?"

"Better now." He grinned at her, intent on focusing on her as a friend. "How's the parenting shift going?"

A gentle smile curved her lips. "We colored this morning and said our A-B-Cs."

"You're the best."

She paused, looking up at him. "What brought that on?"

"I see the way you care for Faith and Joy. The love you shower on them. I'm more thankful than I can say."

"They make love easy."

"On the good days, right?"

She chuckled. "Even on the bad. They stare up at me with those big puppy-dog eyes, and I can't stay mad."

He understood that perfectly. Because when Trinity laughed at his jokes, cared for him and his girls, he couldn't help but feel those little cracks in the armor around his heart. Almost like he was helpless and doomed to fall. *No. Remember, friendship feelings only.*

Trinity shook her head, a look of bemused

amusement tugging a dimple forward. He must have seen that dimple a dozen times but it snared his gaze for a second that lasted almost long enough to be considered a moment.

"Omar?"

He blinked. "Sorry, what?"

She pointed behind him. "Do you want to take a photo with the girls?"

"Sure." He forgot the captain had set up a makeshift photo booth.

They called for the girls to exit the bounce house and made their way to the end of the photo line. He watched as some of the families grabbed the available props to make their pictures more fun.

"Should we use the props?" Trinity asked.

"I was just wondering about that." He looked down. "Girls, do you want to use some props for the pictures?"

"Angel wings!" Joy shouted. She pointed to some white wings laid out on the table nearby.

Omar grabbed them and slid them onto Joy's arms so they could flutter against her back.

"What about you, Faith?" Trinity knelt in front of his daughter.

"I want the halo."

"Two angels," Omar noted. He kissed Faith's cheek as he slid the halo Trinity handed him on top of her head like a headband.

They stepped forward and took their spot in front of the canvas background. The photographer took a few shots, then gave them a number and pointed to a booth. "My assistant can download these and make y'all some copies."

"Thanks, man." Omar shook his hand and led the girls to the printing area.

As they stared down at the printed images, Faith sniffled.

"What's wrong, baby?"

"I happy."

Oh wow. Could three-year-old girls already know about happy tears?

"What are you happy about?" Trinity asked.

"There's a daddy and a mommy in the picture."

Omar stared speechless as the impact of her words settled around him. If he had any doubts he'd done the right thing in marrying Trinity, Faith's words would certainly erase them. His girls needed a mom and Trinity would be that for them.

Seeing how happy his girls were made him glad they married. He just had to remember they could only be friends. The kids were the ones supposed to be benefiting from the convenience, not him. He couldn't let it turn into anything more.

Chapter Thirteen

Today's disaster had completely defeated Trinity. She lay facedown on her bed, unable to move as the horror of the day went through her mind like a movie montage. It all started when Joy had decided screaming at the highest pitch possible was the only way to answer Trinity's questions. Her ears were still ringing.

As if that hadn't been bad enough, Faith had dissolved into meltdown mode, shrieking during snack time, once more deciding ants on a log was *not* acceptable fare. When Trinity had refused to make anything else, the shrieks of *no* ramped up. She was surprised the cops weren't called in for a welfare check between the two shrieking toddlers.

Who knew telling a toddler to sit on the stairs for time-out would cause such a visceral reaction? The depths of despair intoned in Faith's cries almost made Trinity capitulate to her demands of no time-out. *Almost*.

The icing on the cake? Omar wouldn't return from work until noon tomorrow. Granted, he'd have the next three days off as the station got ready to do some weird shift change she didn't understand—even though Omar had tried repeatedly to explain the process to her. No, what worried her the most was he'd be home for three days straight.

Three. Days.

Things between them had been weird lately. Sometimes she'd catch Omar staring at her almost like he had *feelings* for her. And not the kind that had them telling jokes and doing their BFF fist bump. No, the kind that would normally have one singing "Chapel of Love." But since they'd skipped the normal progression and settled for a marriage of convenience, Trinity didn't know what to think.

Surely Omar's feelings hadn't changed. Christine had been his one and only and he *knew* how Trinity felt about romance.

She flinched as her app trilled. Trinity rolled onto her back and stared at the screen. Confusion filled her at the blinking number. Her blood sugar was seventy? Not terrible, but enough for the app to scream for her to eat some food. She stood up.

"Whoa." Trinity held an arm out to steady herself.

Light-headedness was usually the first sign of low blood sugar, but maybe her head only swam because she'd gotten up too fast. For safety's sake, she held on to the railing and headed downstairs for a snack. Maybe she'd drink a little cup of juice or sweet tea to get her number up faster.

Thankfully, the girls were still napping. She had no energy—literally—to handle their antics. Her mouth dropped wide as she saw her lunch on the kitchen table. Hadn't she eaten? She remembered sitting the girls down, strapping them in their seats. What had happened to distract her from actually eating the taco lettuce cups? *Oh yeah, the ants on the log.* No wonder her sugar had dipped low.

She'd have to do a better job of making sure she ate when they did.

After eating and then cleaning up the living room, Trinity shuffled to the wall thermostat in front of the stairs. Why was it so hot in the house? Had the air conditioner stopped working? *74.*

That wasn't hot at all. Omar always set it to seventy when he came home, but she and the girls preferred it a little warm. Still, it seemed unusually hot.

"Mommy!" Faith stood at the top of the stairs, Trinity's cell phone in one hand and the other covering her ear. "It's loud."

"What?" Why did Faith's voice sound so far away?

"The phone is screaming!"

Joy joined her sister, hands over her ears.

Was her app malfunctioning? Trinity looked down at her pod. Nothing was out of order. She took a step toward the stairs, frowning at how heavy her foot was. Then another. Realization flooded her system. Her blood sugar hadn't gone up. Something was wrong.

"Call your daddy," Trinity said before she sank into the darkness.

Omar frowned as his phone vibrated in his pants pocket. He didn't want to look at it since he was in a meeting, but this was the second time it had gone off. Maybe the call was an important one. He slid his cell phone out and his eyes widened. Trinity's app had sent him an alert.

Her blood sugar's thirty?!

"Cap, I need to go." He winced at the look of annoyance on Captain Simms's face. He held up his phone. "Trinity's diabetic and I just received an alert saying her blood sugar is dangerously low."

Just then the station's medical alert system sounded. "Medical attention is needed at 54 Oakview Court. A child called. Mother is unresponsive."

Omar flew out of his seat. "That's my address."

The room erupted in movement as everyone flew into response to handle the call. His heart pounded as he jumped into the bus—*ambulance*—with Spence.

"We'll get there in time, Young. It's in God's hands," Spence offered as he sped out of the garage and onto the street.

Omar wished he could take comfort in that, but God had already taken one wife. What's to say He wouldn't take another? Omar couldn't think like that. *I'm sorry for being so cynical, Lord. Please, have mercy on Trinity. Watch over my family, please.* He swallowed.

Were the girls scared? Crying?

Was Trinity alive?

His heart stuttered and his vision blurred before him.

"Young! Young! You gotta stay calm."

Omar shook his head, flinging the fog away as he drew in a shaky breath. Then another. And another. Each inhale brought sweet oxygen to his system. By the time the bus stopped in front of his house, Omar had his emotions back under control.

He hopped out, racing up the driveway and unlocking the front door with a quickness that surprised him, considering how badly his hands shook.

"Trinity!" Her limp body lay at the bottom of the stairs. He bent down on one knee to check the pulse in her neck. She was alive! "Thank You, God." He wanted to weep with relief.

Spence took over and motioned for Omar to turn around and look behind him. The girls were upstairs, tears streaming down their faces. He rushed up and unlatched the baby gate. "It's okay. She's okay." He wrapped them in his arms, murmuring soothing noises to them.

"Is she dead?" Faith asked in between sniffles.

"She's alive. My friend Spence down there is going to get her feeling better. I'm going to go to the hospital and make sure she's all better, 'kay?"

"I called 9-1-1, like you taught me," Faith cried.

"You did good, baby."

He hauled them up, put one on each hip and jogged down the stairs. Spence and the rest of the crew had already placed Trinity onto the stretcher. Omar ran next door and slowed when Trinity's mom came out of the house.

"What's wrong?" She wrung her hands, her gaze shifting from his to the commotion behind him.

"Trinity's blood sugar is low."

Her mother's face blanched.

"I want to go make sure everything is okay, but the girls are a little shook."

"I'm sure they are." She reached for Joy and

then took Faith. "Go. Let me know as soon as we can come."

"I will, Mrs. Davis."

She shooed him. "Call me Mom now."

"Bye, Mom." He paused and kissed her cheek.

Later he'd sit down and examine the feelings rushing through him at calling yet another mother-in-law Mom. That had been what Nancy urged him to call her.

He hopped into the captain's truck and buckled up. "Thanks."

"No problem. I sent the ladder back to the station, and Spence is already on his way to the hospital. Once I drop you off, I'll head back."

"I appreciate the ride."

"You just take care of your wife. Don't worry about work matters."

Omar nodded absentmindedly. His mind had already dumped all things work related. All he could picture was Trinity's still body draped along the stairs. He prayed she had no bruising or broken bones. Had she fallen going up the stairs or down? From the way her body had been lying on the landing, he'd assumed she'd been going up.

He ran a hand down his face. The unknown was awful. He hated not knowing how she was doing. The lump in his throat felt like his heart had lodged there, stuck by fear.

By the time the captain pulled up to the emergency entrance, Omar's nerves were about frayed. With a thanks, he jumped out of the truck and ran inside, straight to the front desk.

"My wife was brought in via ambulance. Trinity Young."

"Yes, sir, Mr. Young. I'll have a nurse come out for you." The receptionist picked up the phone and alerted whoever was on the other end. She placed the receiver down. "She'll be right out."

He slid his hands into his pockets, staring at the double doors that led to the ER, willing them to open. Finally, a petite blonde woman walked out and met his gaze. "Mr. Young?"

"Yes, ma'am." He followed her through the doors. "How is she?"

"The doctor's in there with her now. He'll give you an update." She paused and pointed to an open door on the right. "She's right in there."

"Thank you."

"Sure thing."

He stepped into the room, shoulders tense and nerves flinging like a water hose gone loose. "I'm Omar Young." He extended his hand out toward the doctor, his eyes fixed on Trinity's still form.

"Nice to meet you, Mr. Young. I'm Dr. O'Malley. Your wife has been in and out of sleep. We've got her numbers climbing up just like they should be."

"What happened?" He couldn't remember the

last time Trinity's diabetes had sent her to the hospital.

"Faulty pod." The doc held up the pod that Trinity had been wearing on her right shoulder. "It hasn't been sending the injections through."

"But I got multiple alerts with different readings."

"I imagine Mrs. Young heard an alert, ate or programmed an injection, but it didn't matter because the pod didn't send the insulin through her body."

Omar frowned. "It's the pod's fault? I mean, she didn't wear it in that location too much or anything?" Why hadn't he taken the time to know the ins and outs of her disease and medical equipment?

Trinity had been diagnosed as a teenager, but she seemed to adapt so easily to meds and treatments. She was always conscious of just how much sugar she ingested. He knew she didn't like it when people asked about her blood sugar levels, but maybe he should have been a little more conscientious.

"How will we know if the other pods are defective?" He couldn't let this happen again. His stomach dropped to his toes just thinking about a repeat visit to the hospital. One with worse outcomes.

The doctor showed Omar what to look for

while a nurse did another blood sugar check. Dr. O'Malley gave a satisfied nod and exited the room. Omar pulled up a chair next to the railing of Trinity's bed and sat down. He rested his forehead on the bed.

This scene joined an awful replay of a similar one. Both times, he'd been visiting his wife. First Christine, now Trinity. This was what he'd been afraid of—losing another love, another wife. Battling through another round of grief.

Lord, a marriage of convenience was supposed to protect my heart, not put it through the wringer.

Since Trinity was his best friend—his oldest friend—it added another spin to the complications. If he ever lost her, he'd lose part of himself. She'd been with him through every up and down life had thrown his way. If Trinity passed away, how would he cope?

Thankfully the faulty pods could be replaced. He would make sure this never happened again, because he'd been in the hospital one too many times for his liking.

Chapter Fourteen

If Omar checked her blood sugar one more time, Trinity would let out a scream to rival Faith's and Joy's. Ever since she'd come home from the hospital, he'd been hovering over her like a helicopter parent. At first, she thought the attention was a little sweet. She knew Omar valued their friendship and seeing him wait on her showed her just how much.

But that was a week ago. Seven whole days since her defective pod had landed her in the emergency room and with a nervous Nellie for a husband. 168 hours' worth of him drilling holes into her being with his stares to make sure she was feeling fine. Okay, not that many. She could subtract time for sleep and the blessed relief that had brought.

The pharmacy and the insurance company were able to send her a fresh set of new pods, without extra charge. And even though she'd checked to make sure they were A-okay, Omar had inspected them as well.

Her numbers were great, and insulin pumped through her body with every programmed injection. Yet Omar kept checking her app *and* his to make sure all the numbers looked the same. He'd peeked over her shoulder at every check of blood sugar and often asked for her to do so again. She had no fruity breath, no sweating, no signs of her blood sugar going too high or too low.

She was perfectly fine.

Yet Omar continued to treat her as if she had *fragile* written across her forehead. Even the girls looked at her differently. Honestly, that change bothered her the most. It broke her heart to see how clingy Joy had become while Faith eyed her from afar, never getting too close. As if she had to wall up her heart and protect it in case another person she loved died.

Trinity wiped at the tear that rolled down her face. If anyone in the house saw her crying, they'd think the end was near for sure. She sighed and turned on the kitchen faucet to wash her hands. Tonight, she would attempt to cook a meal that might have Omar pitching a fit but would make her taste buds more than happy.

The Texas toast pizzas were sure to be a big hit with the girls. They loved pizza, and what could be better than eating it atop a slice of Texas toast? Her mouth watered as she placed the thick slices on a cooking sheet.

"Cooking already, Trin?"

She looked up as Omar walked by her. "Yes. Texas toast pizza."

"Oh yum. I remember eating these at your mom's house." He popped a slice of pepperoni in his mouth, then froze. "Wait a minute. You can't have that."

Here we go. "Of course I can. I'm having a side salad, and I'll program my pod to ensure I get the proper insulin dose."

"Why don't you just stick to the salad?"

"Are you calling me fat?" She stared him down, willing him to see how ridiculous he was behaving.

His eyes widened in horror. "No...no!" He shook his head. "I'm only concerned with your health. Can't you see that?"

She blew out a breath. "Yes, but can't you see I may be a little," she held her thumb and pointer finger a smidgen apart, "irritated from the constant checkup?"

He rubbed a hand down his face and nodded slowly.

"I know you're concerned, Omar. But you have to remember this wasn't because I wasn't taking care of myself. It was the pod."

"But what if it happens again?"

She prayed it didn't but couldn't say another episode wouldn't happen again. "We have to put tomorrow in God's hands. We can't live in fear."

"I know," he murmured.

Trinity reached out and laid a hand on his forearm. "I'm fine. I promise."

What did the look on his face mean? Was he still grieving Christine's death? Overly concerned about her? She wished she could tell, but one thing was certain, it wasn't a happy expression. Without thought, she wrapped her arms around Omar and gave him a hug. The strength of his arms warmed her insides and wrapped her with an assurance of being safe.

"I'd be lost without you, Trinity."

"I'm not going anywhere," she said into his shirt. "BFFs."

"Forever," he whispered.

The urge to rest her head against his chest pricked at her. Heat filled her cheeks, and she pulled back. Her pulse beat a little too quickly for it to have just been a friendly hug. Her thoughts jangled in confusion.

Omar exhaled loudly. "Sorry for being overbearing."

"Forgiven." She forced a smile onto her face. "As long as you let me eat my Texas toast pizza."

He chuckled. "Go ahead. But I'm still checking your pod."

She opened her mouth to protest, and he held a hand up to stop her.

"I just won't do it as much. Fair enough?"

"Fine."

Omar threw the salad into a bowl and added carrots, tomatoes and diced-up cucumbers. Trinity placed the toast in the oven, enjoying the hum of activity in the kitchen.

"Want me to get the girls?" he asked.

"Please." Trinity set the table and moved the salad bowl to the center. All she needed was for the toast to finish cooking and dinner would be served.

She thought about her conversation with Omar. Now that they'd cleared the air, hopefully he'd throttle back his hovering to a mere dip before rotating to the next victim. She shook her head ruefully. Maybe she just needed to get out of the house. She'd been cooped up for too long and since Omar would be going back to work tomorrow, she could return to a normal routine.

Maybe then Omar and the girls would be reassured she was just fine. Joy came rushing into the kitchen, arms out wide for Trinity to pick her up. She bent at the knees and swooped the little girl up.

"Mwah," she said, placing a kiss on Joy's cheek. "You hungry?"

Joy nodded vigorously.

"Good. Dinner's about done." The timer on the oven beeped. "See?" Trinity buckled Joy into her high chair and then got the food out of the oven. The smell of the melted cheese and tomato sauce made her stomach rumble.

Omar walked in with Faith and helped her into the chair. Trinity plated the food, then she and Omar carried the dishes to the table.

"Looks yucky," Faith proclaimed.

Trinity stifled a groan. If anyone would complain, it would be her. "It's pizza."

"Nuh-uh. P-za doesn't look like that."

"It's on toast, sweetie," Omar coaxed.

She scrunched her nose up. Trinity could only pray Faith wouldn't throw a fit. Then again, the threenager seemed to save those for when Omar was at work. Trinity cut up Joy's food as Omar used his child whisperer voice to get Faith to at least try a piece. She eyed the offering on her plate suspiciously but finally took a bite.

"Do you like it?" Trinity asked.

The little girl shrugged, but the way she wiggled in her chair told Trinity the truth. She smiled. Finally, things were getting back to normal. Little girls who would argue over dinner, or

eat it happily (Joy) and a husband—best friend—
who'd agreed to stop hovering.

Every time he closed his eyes, Omar pictured
Trinity unconscious at the bottom of the stairs.
Heard his daughters' cries in the deep, dark recesses of his mind. The memories taunted him,
drove out his peace, and he had no idea how to get
it back. He prayed verses that spoke to incompre-
hensible peace, but his nerves remained shattered.

He'd apologized to Trinity for being overbearing, but honestly, he wasn't sure how to stop.
Even now he wanted to check her blood sugar
and make sure the insulin was doing its job. He
couldn't even enjoy the Texas toast pizza because
his stomach was too busy doing acrobatics as he
watched her without being obvious.

Which was almost impossible. How could he
not watch her? What if something happened to
her the moment he stopped looking? What was
he supposed to do when he returned to work?

Omar blew out a breath and concentrated on
chewing the piece of food in his mouth. His girls'
dinner antics couldn't even help him focus. All he
could concentrate on was Trinity's health.

*Lord God, please bring all my thoughts cap-
tive under the obedience of the Lord Jesus Christ.
I can't keep spiraling and worrying. But I don't*

know how to turn this fear over to You. How do I let go?

He swallowed and pushed his plate away.

"You okay?" Trinity asked, frowning at the food still on his plate.

"Just can't seem to eat."

Her brow furrowed. "Does your stomach hurt?"

"Daddy sick?" Faith asked, eyes widening and tearing up in a matter of seconds.

"No, baby. I'm fine." He leaned over, placing a kiss on her cheek to assure her. "Guess my mind's thinking too much to eat."

Faith stared at him, confusion puckering her lips. "What?"

"Oh, Faith, sweetie, don't say 'what' like that," Trinity lightly scolded. "If you don't hear your daddy, just ask him to repeat that."

"Repeat dat," she snapped out.

Omar bit back a chuckle. Certainly, Trinity had meant it to sound like a respectful request and not a demand from his challenging toddler. He looked at Trinity, and she shook her head as if to say *Toddlers.*

They finished their meal, did their bedtime routine, and soon it was just him and Trinity. Omar wanted to ask her about her blood sugar but a glance at his app showed no alerts. He wondered if there was a way to change the parameters and get all the information she received on her app instead of only alerts. *No. I said I wouldn't be overbearing.*

He sighed, closing his eyes as he sank into the couch cushions.

Footfalls sounded behind him then the sofa dipped as Trinity joined him on the couch. "Tired?" she asked.

"A little."

"You know why?"

He peeled an eye open, turning his head to see. "Why?"

"Stress."

"What stress?" His lips twitched as he closed his eye again.

She lightly shoved his arm. "You know what I'm talking about. You're going to go prematurely gray checking on me twenty-four/seven."

"You're my best friend."

"And don't forget, a grown woman."

"Yeah, yeah, yeah."

She chuckled, and the band that had been squeezing his heart loosened. He really was making last week's episode a big deal. The doctors said it wasn't her fault, just the pod's. *It was the pod's, not Trinity. The pod's, not Trinity.*

Maybe if he could get that stuck in his brain, he'd be able to relax and get back to the status quo. Or maybe he just needed to emphasize their relationship as one of friends and not married friends.

"Want to play Mario Kart?" He eyed Trinity, waiting for her response.

"Sure." A sly grin deepened the dimples in her cheeks. "You ready to lose?"

"Bring it." He powered on the video game console, picked up a controller and handed one to Trinity.

This was normal. This was the old them. He could handle it. Except when Trinity laughed with delight when coming in first, Omar found himself grinning along with her. He had a sense of pride every time he managed to make her smile or laugh outright. Like he'd accomplished something important.

And wasn't that something a husband wanted to do? He wanted to groan in frustration, but Trinity couldn't know the turmoil he was in.

He cleared his throat. "What are your plans for tomorrow?"

"Is this you concerned or curious?"

"Curious." He chuckled despite the aggravation in her tone.

"I was thinking of taking the girls to storytime."

"Fun."

"I hope so. Pray there's no meltdowns."

"No kidding."

The more they talked, the more Omar was able to relax. He didn't know how, but he was hopeful he could remember Trinity was his best friend and nothing more. He just couldn't let their friendship turn into anything else. It was the only way to keep his heart safe.

Chapter Fifteen

Trinity opened the door to All the Spines, the local bookstore that sold new releases and used books. The best of both worlds really.

"Mommy." Joy struggled to turn around in the stroller. "Book?" She pointed toward the children's section.

"In a moment, Joy. I need to find Kris or one of the other employees."

Movement sounded to her left and she turned. Amanda walked down the aisle and smiled at the them. "Good afternoon. A little early for storytime, isn't it?" Amanda checked her watch.

"Actually, Amanda, I wanted to know if y'all are hiring part-time." She held her breath.

She'd been wrestling with the idea since she'd been back home from her health scare.

"Oh." Amanda blinked owlishly behind her thick red-framed glasses. "I'm sorry, but we aren't." She leaned forward. "In fact, someone's getting laid off this week. Sales have been down."

Trinity frowned. "I'm so sorry to hear that." Especially since she needed a way to contribute somehow to the arrangement with Omar. If she had a job, maybe, just maybe, her heart would have room to breathe and keep the protections she'd placed secure.

"Bluebonnet is small and sales in bookstores are down nationally."

"Still. I love this place."

"Well, keep visiting and doing your part."

"We will." Trinity thanked her and pushed the stroller toward the children's section, then parked it out of the walkways.

Where else could she work in Bluebonnet? She couldn't do anything outside of the home full-time. That would defeat the whole purpose of her helping Omar with childcare.

After unbuckling the girls, she helped them each pick out a book, but they quickly became distracted by the puppet show toys. Her cell phone chimed within the diaper bag and Trinity pulled it out to check her notifications. She clicked on the alert from Omar.

I've been at work for two hours and I can't stop worrying. How's your blood sugar? How are you?

I'm fine, Omar.

Are you sure? I can take off work and be there in a jiffy.

And get fired?

Fine, make sense.

Trinity chuckled.

You know I'm fine.

Maybe I do.

Three dots appeared, bouncing on the screen so she waited for Omar to finish the new text.

Rider wants to know if we'd like to go bowling tomorrow.

You won't be tired from your shift?

Nah.

Sure. Who else is going?

Why don't you invite Jalissa?

Will do.

Trinity quickly fired a text off to her friend and waited for her response. When she got an affirmative, she let Omar know. Tomorrow would be fun.

Bowling with two competitive people was *not* fun.

Trinity eyed Jalissa and Rider as they bickered about who stepped over the line. She always thought the line was a suggestion, not a rule you couldn't cross. Omar sat next to her, draping an arm over the back of her chair.

"Do you think they like each other?"

She snorted. "No way. Jalissa doesn't like firefighters."

"What?" Omar jerked back as if he'd been punched. "So, it's not me? It's because I'm a firefighter?"

Her lips twitched. "It might be a little of both. But with Rider, it's one hundred percent his occupation and lackadaisical attitude."

"Eh, I get that. His personality gets under my skin at times."

"Poor baby."

Omar rolled his eyes at her good-natured teasing. "Seriously though, what's her deal with firefighters?"

"Besides their egos?"

"Hey."

She laughed. "Her word, not mine."

"As long as you remember you married one."

Every day. She blinked wondering where that thought came from. Somewhere between *I do* and today, the ring on her finger no longer made her panic. Instead it filled her with a contentment she hadn't realized had been lacking until now. Being a part of the Young household had given her a new purpose. It was almost as if she…*liked* being married. And not married to just anyone, but to Omar.

But he's my best friend

"Well, whatever that is between them," Omar stated, his words breaking into her musings, "I wish they'd hurry up and bowl." He shouted the latter part of the sentence so the two could hear him.

Trinity quickly clamped down on her lips, hiding her laughter from Jalissa and Rider. Jalissa frowned and Rider motioned her forward, reminding her to stay behind the line. Jalissa rolled a strike, throwing her hands up in victory. She stuck out her tongue at Rider, and Trinity lost it. She doubled over at the waist, laughing at her friends.

As she wiped her eyes, she smiled with pleasure. Her mother had been ecstatic to watch the girls so she and Omar could hang out with their friends tonight. Trinity was glad she didn't have to worry about them right now. She wouldn't miss the funny shenanigans between her friends for anything.

Trinity turned to Omar. "I didn't realize bowling was so serious."

"To competitor A and competitor B it is." He shrugged. "I just wanted to get out of the house and do something fun. It's been a while since we hung out just for the fun of it."

"You're right. My days have been filled with kid shows, naps and tantrums."

"Oh, come on. The one I threw the other night wasn't that bad."

Trinity's shoulders shook with laughter. He'd pouted when she beat him in Mario Kart. His facial expression had reminded her so much of the girls, she couldn't help but laugh, which made him mope even more. Nights like this reminded her of why she had so much fun with him. He could always keep her laughing even when she didn't want to.

"Your turn, Trinity."

"Right." She hopped up and grabbed the neon green ball. She lined her feet up to the middle arrow and slowly walked forward, swinging her right arm back and then letting it fly free when she threw the ball forward. The ball spun to the left and landed in the gutter.

She groaned and trotted to the ball return, waiting for a flash of neon green to appear.

"Hey, Trin?"

"Hmm?" She looked up at Omar.

"If you move a little to the right maybe it won't go in the gutter anymore."

Heat filled her face. She'd alternated between gutter balls and knocking down a pin or two. She shrugged her shoulders. "I'm just not that good, but I am having fun. Promise."

"At least let me help you a little."

She picked up her ball and Omar placed his hand on the small of her back. He guided her hand, holding the ball, and goose bumps broke out along her skin. Embarrassment twisted her insides at the reaction. How ridiculous for her to respond in such a way to her friend. Just because she was forgetting the oddness of marrying for convenience didn't mean she had to develop feelings for him.

You're better than that, Trinity.

She willed her mind to remember Jason's face and reopen the old wound of being jilted. To remember the stunned faces of the attendees. How broken she'd felt. The lack of closure she'd dealt with, until finally, Jason had emailed her saying he was sorry but not. Yet even the memories

stung a little less than before, and Omar's soothing voice continued to drone on with instructions
on how to stand and swing.

It was oh so tempting to let her feelings run free
toward romance. To think of the kindness Omar
showed her on a daily basis. The easy rhythm
they'd fallen into taking care of the girls. Like a
unit. *A couple.* But she needed to remember that
if things fell apart this go-around, she wouldn't
be the only one affected. Faith and Joy were in-
tegral to this arrangement. So when Omar asked
if she understood, Trinity nodded and stepped
away from him. She pictured the word *romance*
with a line through it and swung the bowling ball.
Spare!

Omar hadn't felt so relaxed in…well, he
couldn't remember how long. A night out with
friends was just what he needed. No temperamen-
tal toddlers to worry about. No need to have his
mind braced for an alert—medical or parental.
He could clear out his mind and enjoy the company of friends.

Except when he showed Trinity how to bowl,
he'd been struck by the rightness of it all. Them
together, enjoying one another's company, and the
distinct impression that all was right. And when
he pictured home, Trinity was the first person to
come to mind.

For a moment, he'd sunk into the feeling, let the thought settle in like the warmth from a bonfire for Friday night football. He'd been tempted to wrap her in a hug and just be, but she'd shifted away and reality doused him like cold water.

He was a widower. He'd already married the woman of his dreams and lost her when cancer had ravaged her body. There was no need for a repeat of heartache. *But wouldn't it be nice to have a companion again? A wife to love and cherish and who would respect and love you back?*

He swallowed. What did allowing Trinity into his heart mean for the life he'd created with Christine? What would it do to his heart to love and lose again? But Trinity could live well into her eighties.

Maybe developing feelings wasn't such a bad thing?

"Omar?" Jalissa snapped her fingers in front of his face.

He blinked, moving his head away from her fingers. "What did I miss?"

"Want to go grab something to eat?"

"Sure." He looked at Trinity. "You good with that?"

Her lips quirked, the dimple winking in amusement. "I already said so. We were waiting on your vote."

"Oh." He ran a hand across the stubble lining his chin. "I must have zoned out."

"I'll say." Jalissa shook her head. "Hickory's good with you?"

"Oh yeah." He rubbed his stomach. Hickory's had the best barbecue and a dance hall to boot. "I love that place."

"Great. Let's go." Rider grabbed his bowling ball and placed it on a shelf.

One by one, they all followed and after returning their shoes, headed out the door. Hickory's was about a mile away and was sure to be packed. If people weren't cooking at home, they were eating at Hickory's.

When they pulled up to the old warehouse that was now Hickory's, the waiting area only had a couple of families. Maybe they wouldn't have a long wait after all. Omar looked around the building, taking in the sights and smells. Five years ago, Old Man Hickory had bought the place and refurbished it. One side had been outfitted with round dining tables with black-and-white checkered tablecloths. The other held an old jukebox with ample room for dancing on the rubber floor. The industrial piping had been spray-painted white, giving the inside a crisp, clean feel. The live music on the weekends brought the people in droves.

Val seated them at a table in the back of the

room, giving them full view of the space. Omar sat on the left of Trinity as Jalissa took a space to her right, with Rider taking the last empty spot.

"What are y'all ordering?" Trinity asked.

"Barbacoa tacos," everyone said simultaneously, before breaking out in shared laughter.

The slow-cooked shredded beef had a melt-in-your-mouth flavor. Hickory served his on a puffy taco that made Omar want to eat as many as possible. Their server quickly took their orders, returning soon with their cold drinks.

Omar slipped out his cell phone and checked Trinity's diabetes app. *No notifications.*

"I'm fine," she whispered. "I even ordered a diet soda."

"Who can resist a diet Dr Pepper?"

She chuckled. "You."

"What can I say? I'm a purist."

"What are you two whispering about?" Jalissa interrupted.

"We're talking about our drink preference," Trinity piped up.

"Big Red all the way." Jalissa raised the red-colored soda.

Omar felt his mouth scrunch up. It tasted like cotton candy to him. No thanks.

"My favorite too," Rider said, holding his glass up.

"Cute. Y'all have something in common."

Rider rolled his eyes at Omar's comment and he snickered.

Their conversation flowed freely as they ate until they pushed their plates away. Blues and country music had been alternating on the jukebox all night long. Maybe he should get out there and dance.

As if Rider had read Omar's mind, he turned to Jalissa. "Want to dance?"

She shrugged a shoulder. "Sure."

Omar turned to Trinity. "Want to join them?"

"Why not."

A slow song streamed through the speakers, talking about love and marriage, as they took to the floor. The irony wasn't lost on him. Omar cupped the side of Trinity's waist and interlaced his other hand with hers. They'd danced in the past at Hickory's but probably when they were teenagers. *We didn't even dance at our wedding.*

Granted, it hadn't been that type of affair. No fuss, no heart.

He peered into Trinity's eyes. "Tell me something I don't know about you."

"That seems impossible." Lines around her eyes crinkled in amusement.

"Yeah because we've known each other forever."

"Practically."

He shook his head. "There's gotta be something I don't know."

She bit her lip as if searching her memories and twenty-plus years of friendship to find the elusive nugget. "Jimmie Roland was my first kiss."

His insides clenched in a mixture of shock and an emotion he didn't quite want to name. "He was a tool."

A choke of laughter escaped. "I thought he was charming."

"Seriously? How could you date that guy?"

"We didn't actually date." She sighed. "The guy I originally had a crush on started dating someone else and then Jimmie came around. Made me feel beautiful and worthy of another's attention. So when he kissed me, I didn't object."

"But you never dated him." It was more statement than question. An affirmation he desperately wanted to hear. Maybe even *needed* to?

"No. Mama didn't like him, and when she caught us kissing—a very innocent one, might I add—she sat me down and told me why boys like him were trouble."

Strange relief filtered through him. "What reason did she give?"

"Said he was too much into his looks and didn't know they'd fade."

He laughed. "That premature balding at twenty-five proved her point."

"Hey, he's still hanging on to that rim of hair, hoping for a comeback."

Their laughter melded as he guided them around the dance floor. A comment she'd made filtered through the haze of the moment.

"Wait. Who was your first crush if it wasn't Jimmie?" Any why couldn't he seem to remember her old boyfriends?

Trinity met his gaze. She held it a moment then looked away. "You."

He stilled, becoming a roadblock to the couple right behind them. Fortunately, the two merely spared them a glance and kept moving. Omar cleared his throat and resumed dancing. "Why didn't you tell me?" His voice held an odd quality, one even he couldn't quite pinpoint.

She shrugged. "You really liked Christine. I didn't want you to think I was jealous or trying to keep you from happiness."

"Were you jealous?"

A rueful look crossed her face. "Extremely jealous."

His mind filtered through everything he knew about Trinity. How long they'd been friends. How she looked when she was irritated. Angry. Sad. Happy. None of his memories held jealousy in the noggin bank.

"How did I not notice?"

"Maybe you weren't meant to. Think about it.

Y'all married, had two beautiful girls and a wonderful life." She looked down before continuing. "Maybe that wasn't our time."

Were they meant to have one? "I can see your point, but…"

"But what?" She tensed in his arms.

"Well, the summer after sophomore year and before we started out as juniors…"

"The one when Christine moved to town?"

He nodded. "If you remember, she moved here the end of July." He gulped, wondering if he should share what was on his mind. What had been in the past.

"Go on."

"You went away for a week after school ended and came back in June."

"Right. We went to South Padre Island."

"I don't know why, but when you came back, I noticed you were different. All of a sudden my best friend made my palms sweat and my voice crack."

"You *liked* me?" Her mouth dropped open in shock.

Omar nodded, eyeing her warily. He didn't want to cause problems between them, but since she shared about her crush it only seemed fair for him to do so as well. No secrets.

"Why didn't you say anything?"

"You treated me the same. Teased me about my

voice changing. Raced me down to the creek and hogged your tire swing. Nothing you did made me believe you'd be okay if I changed the dynamic between us."

"I…" She bit her lip. "I had no idea. I had such a crush on you that whole summer. When school started and Christine became a permanent fixture, I moved on. I had no choice because I didn't want to be pining over you the entire year. Especially since we were friends."

"I get that. I didn't want to ruin our friendship, which is why I kept quiet."

Silence descended between them.

Omar both wanted and didn't want to know what Trinity was thinking. Instead, he continued to move her around the dance floor as his mind spun. Later, when he was home, he'd think about this newfound information and wonder what to do with it. For now, he'd pretend like nothing earth-shattering had just happened.

Chapter Sixteen

Trinity's heart pounded as she pulled into the fire station's parking lot. Today was their one-month anniversary, if one counted that sort of thing. But after the revelation that Omar had had a crush on her, knowing she'd had one at the same time… well, it all just made the anniversary more prevalent in her mind.

Not to mention she hadn't visited Omar at work as much as she would have premarriage. She'd only been to the firehouse once—for the family day. Somehow, putting on a wedding ring had prevented her from doing something she'd done dozens of times before: joining him for lunch on his shift. Seeing the ring on her finger had made the task appear too wifely, so she'd labeled visits a task to avoid.

But last night, as she'd stared up at the ceiling trying to reconcile all the emotions going through her mind, the need to do something nice nudged her conscience. She'd been so conscious of sticking to the perspective of *friend* not *wife* that she'd distanced herself and lessened her interactions with Omar. Even trying to get the job at the bookstore. All just to spend less time with him? How had she forgotten he was her friend first, foremost and always?

Yesterday's night out had reminded her of that. Well, before he'd dropped the crush bomb, anyway. But she was intent on crossing the bridge to normalcy. She was so tired of feeling awkward about their marriage of convenience. She wanted them back. Their uncomplicated friendship that had been as easy as breathing.

So, with the girls' help, Trinity made brownies with and without nuts, since she remembered one of the new firefighters had a nut allergy, though she couldn't recall who. And because of the captain's health consciousness and her own dieting restrictions, she'd also brought a quinoa salad.

"You girls ready?"

"Yes," they chorused.

Trinity settled them into the stroller and put the cooler tote over the left handle. Traveling with kids seemed to require a lot of time and extra baggage. Every time she was out and passed another mom, she couldn't help but give a head nod in solidarity. They'd packed the kids for an excursion and were battle ready.

Her pulse pounded as she pushed the stroller through the open bay. It seemed unusually quiet. She was pretty sure the guys had lunch at one and it was now half past noon. Had they been called to an emergency?

"Mrs. Young, fancy seeing you here." Rider sauntered over, hands in pockets and a half smirk, half smile on his face.

"Hey, Rider. Where is everyone?"

"We just got out of a meeting."

"And you were the first to hightail it out of there, huh?"

"Oh, well, you know." He shrugged, lips twitching. His blue eyes shined with amusement.

She stifled a chuckle. Rider seemed to flirt the line between good guy and troublemaker.

"Did you come here to see me?"

"Please," she snorted. "We're here to see Omar."

"Oh, I see how it is. No time to joke around with me now that you're married."

"You know it." She shook her head at his antics. "But hey," she tapped him on the arm, "call Jalissa. She's always game for jokes." Not that Trinity would ever stop joking around with Rider. She just wanted to hear what he'd say about Jalissa.

He rubbed his chin. "Maybe."

Movement shifted behind Rider, and Trinity saw the other firefighters idling about the bay. She spotted Omar and waved. A smile lit his face. Was that for her? Her heart dove for her toes as her breath caught in her throat.

Why was her heart doing flips as if it wanted to swoon at the sight of her husband? Was it last night's conversation that brought this change? The fun they'd had every time they were in each other's company? Maybe she needed to have another talk with her heart and the dangers of letting it roam free.

Lord, I don't know how healthy it is for all these feelings to flood my system at once. I'm slightly light-headed and wary.

"Hey, there." Omar squeezed her elbow in greeting.

"Hi," she breathed.

"This is a pleasant surprise." He bent down in front of the stroller. "How are my girls doing?"

"Good." Twin giggles reached her ears.

Of course! He'd been grinning at Faith and Joy, not her. She bit her lip to hide her disappointment, then shook her head inwardly. She shouldn't feel sad; they were *just* friends.

Omar stood once more. "What brings you by?"

"I brought brownies and quinoa for lunch contributions." She tapped the cooler and offered a smile, her pulse still thumping a little too fast despite the talk she'd given herself.

His eyes widened and a hint of a smile ghosted his lips. "Did you?"

She nodded.

"Captain will love that."

Rider peered down at the contents. "Food?"

"Brownies," she replied.

"Sweet." Rider removed the cooler from the stroller handle.

"One has nuts and one doesn't. I went ahead and labeled the containers."

"Smart. Otherwise Bradley will blow up like a puffer fish." Rider puffed out his cheeks in imitation.

Omar grimaced. "Hey, want to go to the bunks?" He pointed behind him. "Day shift cleared out so it should be empty, and we can relax before lunch. Besides, most of the guys should be doing their daily assignments already."

"What's yours?"

"I'll be cleaning the trucks with a couple of the guys after lunch."

"Can we see truck, Daddy?"

"Sure, baby." He unbuckled Faith and then she stood patiently as he unbuckled Joy.

Omar walked them around the truck, pointing out different apparatuses. Trinity's heart flipped in her chest as she watched Omar in his element.

Not just with being a firefighter, but the care and love he showed the girls.

Wasn't there some belief that you could trust a man who treated the women in his life right? If so, then maybe she didn't have to carry the worry that he would hurt her like Jason had.

Lord God, I want to run from these feelings. I don't know what to think about them. And I certainly can't trust myself. After all, I was engaged to a man who had no problem leaving me for something better. Please show me how to guard my heart without messing up our friendship.

She wished her problems could just disappear, but believing in Christ didn't mean her life would be trouble free. She just didn't know if she could count this season of her life as all joy. She certainly hadn't been able to with Jason. Now that she was out of that darkness, she could see the blessing of escaping a man who would run at the first sight of greener pastures.

Now she was married to a man who rushed into trouble, hoping to aid anyone who needed help, to pull them from harm's way with no worry of his own safety. Even though Omar was nothing like Jason and her heart was beginning to light up with one glance from him, Trinity couldn't bring herself to trust her heart with him. She couldn't survive another rejection, especially since her vows tied them together for life.

I'm scared. I don't want to go all in and then have my heart smashed to smithereens. She remembered that deep ache Jason's betrayal had left. How horrified she'd been, knowing she'd have to tell the people waiting in the church that there would be no wedding. But she was already married to Omar and divorce was not an option. *Please help me.*

"Trinity?"

She blinked and met Omar's gaze. His brow wrinkled. Had he called her more than once? "I'm sorry. I was praying."

"Everything okay?"

Not yet, but... "It will be."

He stepped forward. "Do we need to go somewhere and talk? Sans kids?"

"No." She chuckled and squeezed his arm. "I'm good."

"Okay." His eyes darted back and forth, searching hers.

She prayed he could see she was fine. Although she still kind of felt off-kilter, there was no doubt that God heard her prayers. She had no idea how He'd answer them, but He would. It was a promise she would cling to in moments of uncertainty and upheaval. Somehow, some way, God would work everything out for good.

I truly believe that, Lord. Sometimes my brain just needs to hear it more than once.

Omar placed a hand at the small of her back, guiding her as he led them to the back of the bay and up the stairs where the kitchen was located. Hopefully Rider had brought her food offerings straight to the kitchen. Most likely, he stole a brownie or two before setting them out for everyone.

She wondered if he really would get along with Jalissa. The girl didn't like nonsense and Rider seemed to skirt the line a little too much. But who knew?

"You sure are thinking hard over there." Omar glanced at her.

"I was thinking of Rider and Jalissa."

"In what way?"

"Just your idea that they may like each other. I can't help but think she'd eat him alive."

"You did say she hates firefighters."

"But there are moments she's so sweet."

Omar snorted. "To you."

She nodded. "They did dance all last night."

He nodded grudgingly. "Still, Rider's like the poster boy for playing games so why even go that direction? He'd just validate her beliefs."

"True. For some reason though, I can't shake the idea from my mind."

"Tip your head over. Maybe it'll work like an Etch A Sketch."

She didn't know why the thought plagued her

anyway. She had her own troubles to worry about before jumping into someone else's.

A buzzer sounded and red lights flashed throughout the firehouse. Everyone around the table froze. As soon as the mechanical voice gave the alert for a house fire, they sprang into action.

Omar kissed his girls on the forehead and squeezed Trinity's shoulder. "Thanks for coming. See you at the end of shift!"

She nodded, and he hustled after his team.

He climbed into the truck, taking the position behind Rider, who was at the wheel. Omar slid on his headset as Rider sounded the siren and rolled out of the garage. His heart thumped as adrenaline coursed through him. He inhaled and exhaled, counting to ten to center himself.

Lord God, please keep the people who reported the fire safe and away from harm. I pray that You would guide us and help us put the fire out as quickly as possible with no collateral damage. Lord, please see every one of us back to the station with no injuries. Amen.

Dismay soon filled him as they pulled up to the house fire. The yellow farmhouse belonged to Mrs. Ortiz. She always made tamales for the church potluck. He hopped down from the truck, rushing around to the other side to receive his assignment from the captain. Most likely he would be on search-and-rescue with Bradley.

Captain Simms's grim face greeted him. "Young, Bradley, search-and-rescue. No one has come out of the home, and the police haven't confirmed if the place was empty."

Omar nodded and looked to Bradley. "Ready?"

"On your six."

He grabbed the Halligan and headed for the front door, prying it open. A wave of heat hit him. Omar stepped back, eyes squinting to see through the waves of fire and smoke. "Hello!"

Crackling filled his ears amid the roar of the fire. The stifling heat pushed against him with every step. He called out for Mrs. Ortiz once more but heard nothing.

"Bedroom," Bradley called.

Omar nodded as the firefighter veered to the left to check the other part of the house. He continued forward, glancing up every few feet. As he stepped into the kitchen area, a crash sounded behind him. He whirled around, apprehension coursing through him at the scene before him. Part of the ceiling had fallen, blocking his exit.

He pressed his comms. "Ceiling caved in between living room and kitchen. Need another exit."

"Exiting the premises with homeowner." Bradley's voice echoed in his comms.

"Captain?" Omar called, repeating his exit request.

"Back door in the kitchen. You see it?"

Omar scanned the area and sighed with relief. Nothing worse than being trapped in a burning building with no viable exits. "Copy."

"Homeowner said no other occupants."

"Copy." He went around the dining table and headed for the door.

Time slowed as a clamor filled his ears. He looked up and ducked to roll as soon as he saw the ceiling come crashing down.

But it was too late. His body hit the floor and something heavy fell on him. He coughed, breath trapped on an inhale. *Don't panic. Remember your training.* Omar shoved at the material over him, but the roof refused to budge. He was pinned and surrounded by a fire intent on devouring everything in sight.

Lord, help!

"I'm down." His breathing grew labored. Had he hit the comms button hard enough? Did anyone hear him? He couldn't tell if he'd injured his ribs or if the roof was keeping him from taking a full breath. Whatever the cause, pain laced each breath.

"Young, did you exit?"

"No," he croaked. Could the captain hear him? He knew for sure he pressed the comms this time.

"Young?"

"Kitchen," he rasped, trying to add more volume to his voice. He was running out of air. Something was wrong.

This wasn't a simple piece of roof piled on him. He'd injured himself. Had to be a broken rib, right? A sharp pain speared him, and he wheezed. If only he could get a decent breath of air.

Lord God, don't let me die here all alone.

How could he have gone from eating lunch with his girls to this? A picture of Trinity rose in his mind. Her beautiful brown skin. The braids she always styled in different ways. Those dimples that made him grin in response. And the feeling of home she'd created. He'd been ignoring the feelings in his heart for her, afraid to dishonor Christine and risk his own heart. Was it too late?

His eyes grew heavy and the sound of the fire raged.

Lord, please don't take me from my girls—all my girls—right now.

Please...

Help...

Chapter Seventeen

Trinity couldn't focus. Ever since Omar had left the fire station, her mind had been a mess. Was he okay? Was the fire serious? Normally he'd text her throughout the day and tell her about the calls they got. This was different. She'd actually heard the alarm go off for the fire. An *actual* fire. Not a cat stuck up a tree or someone in need of an EMS. He'd been called to put out a *fire*.

Why was her stomach churning like a stormy sea? This wasn't Omar's first fire and certainly wouldn't be his last. But this *was* the first fire he'd been called to since they'd been married. Once more, marriage took something that was a simple fact and added layers of complications.

Lord, please, please keep Omar and the rest of the guys safe. Please bring Omar home to us.

She tapped her lip as she paced around the living room.

"Mommy, color." Faith frowned and pointed to the black-and-white sheet on the coffee table.

Joy sat next to Faith already scribbling away on her paper.

"Sorry, sweetie. I was thinking."

"No think. Color."

Trinity chuckled and sat on the floor, picking up a crayon. The girls loved making crafts or simply coloring in the afternoon. She thought it would be a good idea for them to each color a picture for Omar to hang in his work locker. Only she couldn't keep her mind from seeing him rush out of the station.

She outlined the rose petals on her sheet and filled the space in with a red crayon. If Trinity couldn't clear her mind, at least she could keep her hands occupied instead of gripping her cell phone and willing it to ring. Omar would let her know how he was as soon as he was able.

Lord, please just make it sooner rather than later.

Her skin tingled with apprehension as if ants marched up and down her arms, intent on torturing her. A knock sounded and she jumped, laying a hand over her heart. "Oh, that scared me."

Joy giggled.

"Funny, huh?"

She nodded and Trinity stood. "Be right back." A look through the peephole showed her mother, so Trinity opened the door and gestured for her to come in. "Hey, Mama. What are you up to today?"

"I'm driving up to Waco and wanted to know if you and the girls could come along."

She bit her lip. She'd hate to leave without hearing from Omar but obviously coloring wasn't keeping her well-enough occupied. "I suppose so."

"Don't sound too enthused." Her mother propped her hands on her hips, hurt furrowing her brow.

"Sorry, Mama. I was just thinking about Omar." She told her about the fire and the worry clawing at her, just not in those exact words.

"Oh, sweetie. Waiting is always terrible. Come with me. A little shopping will get your mind off things and release some of that stress."

Maybe she was right. Trinity nodded. "Okay."

"Go on and grab the girls' stuff, so we can hop to it."

"Right." Trinity clapped her hands. "Girls, let's clean up our mess. We're going to hang out with Grandma today."

Faith's bottom lip poked out. "But I not finished."

"Let her finish, Trinity. I can wait a little bit."

Faith beamed and bent over her picture, tongue poked out in concentration.

Another knock sounded on the door.

"We're never this busy." She opened the door and her stomach dropped to her toes.

"Trinity." Rider licked his lips, a look of hesitation on his face. "You wanna come out on the porch and talk?"

There wasn't a trace of soot or grime on him. He looked impeccable in his Bluebonnet FD uniform. So why did her brain sound an alert of alarm?

"No." Her heart thudded in her ears as she gripped the doorknob. How was she supposed to hear what he had to say if the roar in her ears didn't dull? She drew in a shaky breath. "Where's Omar?"

"Trinity, you don't want the girls to hear this."

His words were like ice water, and she snapped out of the coma-like trance seeing him had put her in. She stepped out onto the porch, shutting the door behind her.

"Where is he, Rider?"

"He's at the hospital. He was injured."

"But he's a-alive?" Her heart froze as if waiting to beat with a positive response.

"Yes, ma'am."

A whoosh of air left her lips as her knees trembled. "What happened?"

"Ceiling caved in and trapped him underneath it."

Oh no. She covered her mouth, begging the

contents of her stomach to stay in. Fighting for composure, she looked Rider right in the eyes. "How bad is he hurt?"

"When I left, they were treating him for smoke inhalation, broken ribs and possible punctured lung."

Her breath frayed at his pronouncement. "Did he get burned?"

"No."

A tear slipped down her face. Trinity wrapped her arms around her waist as she tried to form a coherent thought. What she wanted more desperately than anything was for Rider to be wrong. "Oh, Omar."

"I came to bring you up to the hospital."

"Thank you. I just have to tell my mom." She gestured blindly toward the door.

"Take a deep breath, Trinity."

She inhaled. Exhaled. Repeated the deep breaths until the panic receded to functional levels. "I'll be right back."

Rider nodded. "I'll be out here waiting."

"Thank you," she murmured.

She hurried inside to grab her purse from the entry table.

"What's going on?" Her mother stopped by her side, laying a hand on Trinity's shoulder.

"Omar's been injured," she whispered. A quick peek at the girls told her they were oblivious to the turmoil. She turned toward her mom. "Could you watch Faith and Joy for me?"

"Of course." Her mom's brow furrowed. "I'll call the prayer chain."

"Thank you. Could you call Rock too?" At her mom's nod, Trinity continued, "I don't know how long I'll be." Or what would happen once she hit the hospital.

His list of injuries sounded awful. She bit her lip, exhaling a shaky breath.

"Did Rider say how bad the injuries are?"

She gulped. "He said he may have a punctured lung."

"Lord, have mercy," her mother whispered, covering her mouth with her hand. "Update me as soon as you can."

"I will." She wrapped her arms around her mom, savoring the comfort that only a mother could provide. "Thank you, Mama."

"Anytime, sweetie. Go take care of your husband."

Trinity rushed out of the door and followed Rider to his truck. Her hands shook as she struggled to get her seat belt on.

"Breathe, Trinity. Young will be okay. He's the toughest man I know. Plenty stubborn." He winked.

"I appreciate that." If Rider thought Omar would be okay, maybe it would be true. Maybe all the thoughts inside her brain were just magnified because she hadn't seen him yet.

"Sure thing. Now that you and Young are hitched, we've got your back. Firefighters take care of their own."

A strained laugh eased out of her. Her mind raced a million miles as she tried to brace herself. She was sure she'd fall apart once she saw Omar in that hospital bed.

Lord God, please don't let me. I need to be strong for him.

She took a calming breath and glanced at Rider. "Did you see him?"

"I did." Rider glanced at her before looking back at the road.

"Could you paint me a clear picture, so I won't be shocked when I walk in there?" Her hands twisted in her lap.

Rider hesitated a moment. "Uh, sure. He was covered in ash earlier, but I'm sure they've cleaned him up by now. He had some scratches, but the worst areas are the things you can't see—the lung and the ribs."

She didn't know if that was a good thing or not. "Okay. Tubes?"

"Oxygen one and standard IV was all I saw. Try not to worry."

"Kind of hard not to when you say my husband could have a punctured lung." Her stomach dipped. That sounded so *awful*.

Her husband was lying in a hospital bed right now. Not just her best friend, but *husband*. The man she'd pledged her life to, and the one who had wormed his way into her heart in unexpected ways.

Why is this happening, Lord? I just don't understand it.

They'd been through so many little ups and downs in their short month of marriage. Her brain couldn't wrap around the fact that Omar was injured. She still didn't feel recovered from marrying Omar. She'd gone from not wanting to depend on any man to having to marry for the sake of insurance. And now...

Now she depended on Omar for a lot more than insurance for her insulin. The companionship, doing life together on a daily basis. As for her heart...she didn't want to examine the romantic feelings she'd been feeling lately.

What if his injuries were more serious than Rider was telling her? What if he suffered from complications? What would she do? How could she live a life without Omar?

Her breath hitched and tears pricked her eyes. *Don't cry, don't cry, don't cry.* She needed to stay strong. Her mama always said "don't borrow trouble" and surely thinking worst-case scenarios was doing so.

Lord, silence my mind and calm my heart. I place Omar in Your hands. I can't control what happens. But I ask that You heal him this side of heaven. In Jesus's name. Amen.

A whooshing sound and an incessant beeping noise penetrated the haze surrounding Omar. He shifted, wincing at the sharp pain in his chest. Why did his upper body feel like an anvil had been dropped on him? Poor Wile E. Coyote.

His eyes fluttered as memories assaulted him. He'd been trapped. Pinned by a roof and surrounded by fire. Couldn't even breathe. Come to think of it, sucking in air still hurt. He opened his eyes and grimaced at the bright light.

A hospital.

He had to be in one. Why did they feel the need to blind people? You'd think they'd dim the light when a patient was sleeping. He squinted up at the ceiling, taking inventory of his senses. He could feel his fingers, move his toes. Just couldn't breathe too well, albeit, better than before.

"You're awake."

The soft whisper was like the sweetest symphony. Slowly, he turned his head. *Trinity.*

Concern etched lines into her forehead and worry lines curved around her lips.

"Hey, beautiful."

Her lips tipped into a crooked smile and those dimples peeked at him. "Beautiful, huh? They must have you on some good painkillers." Her breath shuddered out and her voice lowered. "I'm so glad you're okay. Do you need some ice chips? Should I call a nurse?"

"No," he rasped as dryness clawed at his throat. "What day is it?"

"Tuesday."

He'd missed a whole day? "What's wrong—" His breath shuddered. He battled against the pain as he drew in another breath.

"Shh." Trinity placed a finger on his lips. "You've got a broken rib, a punctured lung, some smoke inhalation and a bruised body. Just rest. There's no need to talk."

But there was. He needed to tell her how he felt lying beneath part of the ceiling, thinking he wouldn't see tomorrow. Wouldn't see her.

"Trinity." He gasped as the sharpness dug deep. Maybe she was right. Surely, she wasn't going anywhere. His eyes widened. "The girls?"

"My mom's watching them."

He sank back into the hospital bed. He hated feeling so weak but trying to talk even that little bit had taken a lot out of him.

Thank You, Lord, for giving me another day

on this earth. If I wasn't so tired, I'd throw a fist in the air.

He sighed as Trinity stroked his head. She'd never been this demonstrative before. Then again, this was the first time he'd been laid up in a hospital bed. His eyelids fluttered as her movements continued to soothe him.

"Stay?" he whispered.

"I haven't left yet."

His lips twitched into a smile, quickly turning to a frown as another wave of pain hit. He wanted to thank her. Wanted to tell her how much she enriched his life. Only his eyelids grew heavy with each stroke of her hand.

Tomorrow.

He'd tell her how he felt and how glad he was they married. Maybe she'd even bring the girls to see him. They had to be worried, but now wasn't the time to figure all of that out.

Tomorrow.

Chapter Eighteen

Trinity stretched her arms into the air, thankful it was morning. She didn't know who the hospital thought they were fooling, but the couch-bed combo in Omar's room was not comfortable. It was akin to lying on a slab of concrete. Every muscle screamed in protest as she sought to stretch them.

As much as she wanted to stay with Omar and comfort him, she might have to pass on another overnight stay. Her body was too old for a third night on the couch and too weary from the events that had brought them here. She stood, wincing as her body's cracks and pops mimicked a famous breakfast cereal.

She peered at Omar resting in the hospital bed. His dark lashes fanned his face and a look of peacefulness rested on him. He'd been pretty moody and restless last night until the doctor prescribed a different narcotic. Now pain was absent from his features. She hoped his sleep had been better than hers.

Moving to stand by his side, Trinity listened to the symphony of the machines in the room.

Lord, I could have lost him. A lump grew in her throat as she remembered Rider knocking on her door. *Thank You so much for saving him and keeping the others safe as well. It's a blessing no one else was injured, not even the homeowner. Thank You, Jesus.*

She bit her lip. *I know You created Omar to protect others. He's been doing it since childhood, but yesterday was a bit much for me.* Tears pricked her eyes as her breath shuddered out.

All this time, she had been guarding her heart, but it had all been for naught. She loved Omar. Loved him with every beat her heart took. Yesterday had shown her how much when she thought about the possibility of him not surviving his injuries. And even though her mind calmed now that she admitted it, fear encased her, shrouded her thoughts and had her wishing for cover.

What if Omar didn't return her love? What if she told him and he rejected her? She'd promised him that if he said *I love you* she would take it as friendship and nothing more. But she wanted more. Wanted to be able to spill out her feelings and have him return them. To cherish her. To choose *her*.

Tears threatened to spill over. Marrying him had seemed so simple. Live in his guest bedroom. Get health insurance to ensure her diabetes remained in control. All while taking care of the girls when Omar worked. Not once had she thought her heart would get so firmly involved that what had been so straightforward would become more tangled than barbed wire.

Omar would always be her best friend, but not being able to claim him as a true husband—the thought was unfathomable. A tear slipped down her face and she swiped at it.

When she'd texted her mom with the first update, Trinity had asked her to simply tell the girls Omar and she would be back in a couple of days. She hoped that would remain the case. When would the doctor make his rounds today? Was Omar healthy enough to come home?

Trinity needed a long, hot shower and a change of clothes. She couldn't go a third day in the same ones, which meant she'd have to go home and face those precious children and let them know their father had gotten hurt. How did you tell little kids that?

Would they understand?

Would they fear he wouldn't come back like their mother and grandmother?

She groaned, rubbing the center of her forehead. Another round of aspirin should take the ache away and help push back the beginnings of another headache. Too bad it wouldn't ease the tension in her neck or the knots from her shoulders.

Or the pain in her heart.

The door pushed open and a nurse entered.

"Good morning, Mrs. Young." The nurse spoke just above a whisper. "How'd you sleep?"

"I slept." Trinity sent a discreet look at her badge. Last night had been a blur, and she couldn't remember what the lady's name was. The badge read *Jen.*

Jen smiled. "And Mr. Young?"

"Peaceful now." Trinity motioned to the bed. "The pain meds really helped."

"That's exactly what we want to hear. I'll be doing vitals before I get off shift. Do you need anything?"

"Oh, no. I'm probably going to leave soon and get a change of clothes. Do you know what time the doctor will make his rounds?"

"Probably around nine, nine thirty." Jen laid the stethoscope on Omar's chest.

"How's his breathing sound?"

"Much better. Not as labored."

Thank You, Lord. "Do you think the doctor will release him today?"

"I'm betting your guy will be here for a couple of more days."

Trinity nodded, not knowing what else to say. Disappointment cloaked her, but at the same time, she wanted him healthy. Whole.

The nurse rested her hands on the bed rail. "If you want to go home and freshen up before coming back, shift change is the best time to do it. Plus, it'll give Mr. Young more time to rest."

"Okay. I'll do that, then." A good teeth brushing and shower would make a world of difference.

A low moan filled the room. Trinity moved to Omar's side, brushing a hand down the top of his head as his eyes fluttered. A machine beeped.

"I think he's due for more pain meds." Jen checked the computer. "Yep. Be right back."

Trinity nodded absentmindedly, focusing all of her attention on Omar. Her heart beat erratically as she waited to see how he felt. Finally, his eyes opened and searched the room, softening as they landed on her.

"Morning," he mumbled.

"Morning. How are you feeling?"

"Like a house fell on me."

She didn't know whether to laugh or cry, so she shook her head instead. Trust him to make a joke. "Do you need some water?"

"Please."

She grabbed the hospital mug with ounce markings and angled the straw toward his lips.

After taking a sip, he sighed. "That feels good."

"You probably have medicine mouth on top of sleep mouth."

"Attractive, huh?" He grinned, and her cheeks heated.

Since when did he flirt with her? She held in a sigh, remembering he was on narcotics. His feelings weren't like hers. She bit her lip to keep the tears away.

"Hey, you okay?" Concern flashed in his eyes.

Her heart hurt, but she couldn't tell him that. Instead, she kneaded her lower back, noting the physical pain she'd been experiencing. "Sore."

"Lovely bed you had there, huh?"

"Five star."

He chuckled but quickly breathed a hiss of pain.

She laid a hand on him. "I'm so sorry." She shouldn't have made a joke.

"It's okay. I'm just sore too." He wrapped his hand around hers and squeezed.

Warmth filled her heart, and she jerked her hand back. She shouldn't feed into his kindness while he was on pain meds.

Trinity cleared her throat. "I was about to leave and grab a change of clothes." She stared at the door, hating the way her insides were all twisted up.

"I'll be here. I'm assuming the doc won't let me leave today."

"No. Jen, the nurse, said probably a couple more days in here."

He nodded. "Could you bring the girls with you when you come back?"

And let them see him like this? It was already destroying what little hold she had on her emotions. What would it do to the girls? "Do you think it's a good idea?"

"I do. They need to know I'm okay. Just sick. They'll understand."

She exhaled quietly. "Okay, I'll bring them."

Omar cupped the side of her face. "Are you sure you're okay?"

The urge to lean into his touch flooded through her. But she couldn't. This wasn't real. He didn't love her like she wanted him to. "I'm just fine." And she would be as soon as she sobbed her guts out in the shower…or the car if she couldn't hold them in that long.

Thankfully her parents had dropped it off for her. It would make for a fast getaway.

"All right." He withdrew his hand.

Part of her wanted to grab it back. To hold on to it and him until…*until* he realized that them together, in love, was right. That their time was now, and love could last a lifetime. Only she knew Christine was his one and only. Despite the precautions she'd taken, hurt and rejection were a confession away. She needed to get out of her head and away from the man who made her feel way too much.

"I'll be back soon."

"I'll be here."

She fled the room, rushing down the hall, and praying for composure the entire time.

Omar held Faith close as she curled up against his uninjured side. Trinity had the great idea to let the girls lie with him on the hospital bed a bit with the promise of being still. She was afraid they'd jar him or accidentally hit his broken rib if she let them interact as usual.

He only wished he could convince Trinity to curl up next to him too but she had her armor on in full force. She probably thought he hadn't noticed the distance she'd put between them, but she'd be wrong. From the moment she'd jerked away from him and rushed to "change"—like the hospital didn't provide toiletries for loved ones. Plus, he knew her mother could have easily brought a change of clothes and the girls for a visit.

But he'd give her the space she wanted while he was laid up in the hospital. However, once he came home…that was a different story altogether. They needed to discuss why she felt the need to run. Were the emotions between them getting too real for her? Was she scared he wouldn't return them?

Because his brush with death had revealed just how much he cared about Trinity. Only now, he was worried his desire to never hurt her would prove to be false. He was a firefighter. Danger was in the job description and if Trinity fell in love with him, would she one day bury him? Would he put her through the same kind of heartache that he'd already experienced in Christine's passing?

Could he do that to her? Ask her to love him until death…not knowing if it would come sooner rather than later?

"My turn." Joy wiggled in Trinity's arms, pulling his attention from his thoughts and onto his children.

"Okay, baby." He kissed Faith's forehead. "Time to switch out, buttercup."

"All right, Daddy."

Trinity helped Faith down, and then placed Joy carefully by his side.

"Hi, Daddy," Joy whispered.

Oh, how he loved his girls. Nothing could ease life's aches more than a smile from a child. "Hey, baby girl. How you are?"

"Sad."

"How come?"

"Cuz you hurt." She looked at him, an exasperated look on her face better fit for an adult.

He held back a chuckle, though more for preventing pain than laughter.

"Where's your booboo?"

"My ribs." And lungs, but she probably wouldn't understand that.

Joy kissed his cheek. "All better."

His heart melted. *Oh, Joy.* His kids could be the highlight of his day when they weren't driving him completely mad with toddler meltdowns.

After a few minutes of quiet, Joy sat up. "Mommy, you kiss Daddy and make it all better."

Trinity ducked her head, peering at him beneath her lashes. What was she thinking? He wished he could ask her, but there was so much to sort. Instead, he shifted so she could lay a kiss on his cheek. She did so quickly and then stepped back, eyes roving around the room and looking everywhere but at him.

How complicated everything had become. He opened his mouth to say something, anything, to break the tension, but a knock on the doorjamb diverted his attention. Rock stood in the doorway, peering into the room.

"Rock, come on in." He motioned for his father-in-law to enter.

"I don't want to bother y'all." He shuffled a few steps, his brow furrowed as if he'd disturbed them.

"Not at all." Trinity gave Rock a side hug. "The girls and I were just stopping by to say hi." She switched her attention to Omar. "How about I get the girls some *l-u-n-c-h* while you and Rock have a visit?"

"Thank you."

"Sure." She took the girls by the hand. "Let's go find the cafeteria."

"Will we come back?" Faith asked.

"After we have a snack or something, 'kay?"

The girls nodded and followed Trinity out of the room and down the hall.

Omar exhaled and looked at his father-in-law. "Have a seat, Rock."

"How ya feeling?" Rock lowered himself stiffly into a chair.

"Sore. Better than yesterday."

"I gotta admit, you put my ticker into a spin when I heard the news."

Omar grimaced. "I'm so sorry." He sighed. "I imagine a few people were nervous." The guys from the firehouse had been down to check on him intermittently and Rider had been texting him every few hours to make sure he was okay.

The guy had his good moments.

"The prayer chain at church was activated, and

I had a flood of calls at home. Everyone was happy to hear you're doing better."

"I certainly appreciated the prayers." He stared at Rock, wondering if it was a good idea to ask his father-in-law's advice on this particular subject.

Rock placed his folded-up hands on his stomach. "Something you want to talk about?"

"Maybe." Omar stared at the empty doorway. Trinity would probably be a while with the girls. His gaze shifted back to his father-in-law. "I think I'm in love with Trinity."

"You think?" Rock's eyebrows hiked up.

Omar couldn't determine the tone of his voice. "Should I not talk about her with you?"

"Depends on your intentions. Are you asking advice or just telling me how it is?"

"Advice, definitely. You're one of the wisest people I know. I value your opinions and know you wouldn't steer me wrong."

Rock nodded. "Continue, then."

Omar let out a breath, shifting to get more comfortable. "Getting injured kind of shifted my perspective. Had me thinking about how we started this marriage and where I'd like it to go."

"Makes sense. Facing your mortality often does that."

"That's just it. I could die. I don't mean now, but being a firefighter certainly raises my chances."

Rock dipped his head. "And that concerns you?" At Omar's nod, he continued. "In what way? You've always known the safety concerns."

"Of course. Kind of hard not to when we run into burning buildings. But this time was different."

"Were you worried about making Trinity a widow?"

"In the beginning, I fought against feeling that caring for Trinity was somehow a violation of my vows to Christine."

Rock nodded. "I wondered if you felt that way. You seemed to put a lot of weight on being just her friend."

Omar's gaze shifted to the doorway. Still empty. "It was a struggle for a while. I had to reconcile that creating a new life didn't mean I forgot her. Didn't mean I wouldn't make it a point for the girls to remember her."

Rock's eyes glazed over. "Very true. And you know I'll make sure my grands know how much their mama loved them."

Omar smiled.

"But continue on." Rock motioned.

"When I was pinned under that roof, my feelings for Trinity kind of came front and center. But it wasn't until I had time to lie here and think that I wondered about the future. How would she survive if I died? I've never wanted to hurt her.

Jason's abandonment caused so much pain in her life. I would never want to leave her in a similar state."

"And what if you don't? Hmm? Ever wonder what happens if y'all live to a ripe old age? Live long enough to see grandchildren and great-grandchildren? To see the legacy of your love?"

Omar swallowed. "But I could die, Rock. And so could she."

"Sure could. And I could die tomorrow. Will that keep you from visiting me and doing life with me?"

"No. You're my father-in-law. Like a second father to me."

"I love you too, son." Rock chuckled. "One thing I've learned living on earth is that I can't control a single thing. I can't prevent my loved ones from passing." His eyes watered. "But what I can control are my own actions. How I love every person God's placed in my life. How I share that love with the time He's allotted me."

Omar listened with care to the wisdom Rock was sharing. "But loving her affects more than just me, Rock."

"Sure does. Shows your girls how a woman should be cherished. Shows the relationship of Christ and the church. Yep, your actions affect many."

He had to resist the urge to chuckle. Rock knew

what Omar had meant and of course put his wise twist on it.

"Let me ask you this, son."

"Okay."

"If you could have seen that Christine would die when she did, would that have stopped you from asking her out?"

Omar's mouth dropped open in shock. Not what he'd imagined Rock would ask him in a million years.

His father-in-law rose, knees cracking with the movement. "Meditate on that a bit and then you'll know what to do." He softly patted Omar's shoulder. "I'll see you tomorrow, 'kay?"

"Thanks, Rock."

"Think nothing of it."

But thinking was all Omar would be doing.

Chapter Nineteen

A week.

One week had passed since Omar had come home from the hospital to rest and recover from his accident. His recuperation had been *nothing* like Trinity had expected.

For one, she'd assumed there would be a massive amount of time spent waiting on him— bringing all his meals to his room, cleaning up after him, etc. Not that any of that was necessarily a bad thing. She wanted to help him. *Needed* to. If she couldn't express her feelings with words, then certainly expressing them in deeds would alleviate the building pressure.

However, she hadn't expected her emotions to vacillate between wanting to be closer and maintaining a distance that would shield her heart from potential hurt. Part of her wanted to shower Omar with love, and the other half kept waiting for him to reject her outright. Which, in a way, he had.

Omar had been more subdued this past week, keeping to himself, retiring to his room earlier than normal. Gone were the moments of playing video games or streaming a movie and talking. She'd been hoping the change was due to his injuries and the need for his body to heal. She couldn't begrudge that necessity, but Trinity was starting to wonder if it was something else. Surely, he hadn't figured out that she was in love with him. If he had and didn't love her back, well, the thought was too painful to consider.

Trying to escape her thoughts, Trinity grabbed the baby monitor and a bottle of water. Maybe a bit of vitamin D would clear the cobwebs that were her thoughts. And since the girls were napping—Omar as well—there was nothing but peace and quiet surrounding her as the Texas sunshine beckoned from beyond the front porch awning. She inhaled, hoping to clear her mind, but it was no use.

She swallowed, remembering how Omar had made the kids laugh at lunchtime. She'd looked at him and love had overflowed from her heart. Watching the sweet moment between father and children had the words begging for release. Only the imagined look on his face had kept her silent. She'd cry if she said those three precious words and he assumed it was meant out of friendship and not a forever kind of love.

Just saying that in her mind made her heart hurt with the pain of rejection. She straightened her back, lifting her chin. Little movements to help her gather strength to be honest. To admit her feelings to Omar.

And just like that, a whoosh of fear filled her and raised the hair on her arms. *Lord, I couldn't stand it if he said he didn't love me. He's been my best friend for so long. The relationship has been the easiest, most natural thing in the world. But if I change the status quo and he runs away horrified, how will I cope?*

Because there was really no place to hide in the house. It's not like she could hide in the bathroom like other moms. She had to share it with Joy and Faith. The front porch was her only retreat. Texas sunshine and conversation with the Lord would have to help her beat the fear that breathed down her neck.

Lord, I just want to get through life with no drama. No upsets. Just a simple life. This fear is clawing at me, trying to drag me into darkness. I thought getting over Jason meant that I was whole once more.

But who was she fooling? Willingly entering a marriage of convenience to protect her heart was a sign she hadn't overcome the fear of rejection. It was why she couldn't admit to Omar the depth of her feelings. Why whenever he neared, her breath hitched, and an intense ache took up residence in her chest. *Feeling* had become too much.

Be strong and of a good courage; be not afraid, neither be thou dismayed: for the Lord thy God is with thee whithersoever thou goest.

A tear slipped down her cheek as she recalled the sweet verse from Joshua. Their church Bible study group had printed the verse on their handouts last Sunday. It had been the verse of the day on her phone's Bible app. In the past, Trinity had always recited it with a knowing smile of how good the Lord was—*is*. But knowing He was with her didn't quell the fear this time.

Could she really be strong? Have courage? Not fear? Not be dismayed if Omar didn't return her affections?

The call seemed too much to ask of a person. Especially since she sat here, trying to keep tears from falling and a sob from ripping free. She hurt. She ached. She feared.

Lord, can You help me?

"Trinity? You okay?"

She wiped her face and looked up at Omar, forcing her lips upward and faking a calm outward appearance she didn't feel. "Hey. That was a fast nap."

Not nearly long enough. Please don't sit by

me. It was getting hard to maintain her distance and not give in to the closeness her heart needed.

Omar eased his weight onto the porch swing cushion, angling toward her. "Couldn't sleep. I feel tired, but my eyes refused to close."

"I hate when that happens." Lately, her mind had been intent on picturing Omar looking disgusted as she pledged her love. Definitely a reason to keep her eyes open at night.

"Hmm." His eyes traced a path that mirrored the salt tracks down her face. "What's going on in that head of yours?"

The soothing tone of his voice touched her like a caress of the wind. *Fight it.* She couldn't tell him how she felt, but when he acted concerned— no, was *genuinely* concerned—her heart had no defense.

Trinity needed to change the subject. "Do you want me to get you some pain meds? Maybe that will help the pain recede enough to get some rest."

"I don't hurt, Trin. But that's beside the point. Why were you crying?" Frustration furrowed the lines in his forehead.

"Right, no meds."

"Trinity."

Her breath caught and another chip of her armor crumbled at her feet at the concern in his voice. "I…" She swallowed, hating the ache that filled her throat.

Omar studied her. "Please, *talk* to me. We've always been able to share."

And wasn't that the crux of it? She couldn't get advice from her best friend because she'd fallen in love with him. She needed to deflect, but how? "I can't believe how badly injured you were, Omar."

Her heart would not have recovered if she'd lost him.

"But I'm on the mend with no lasting damage." He offered a smile as if to ease her worries.

"But you'll return to work and run right into another burning building."

Lines deepened farther. "Of course I will. It's my job, Trinity."

"And that's the problem." Among many, but the only one she was willing to focus on.

"My job?" His jaw dropped.

"It could kill you." But not as much as being silent was hurting her.

"Lots of things can—"

She spared him a look, asking him with one glance to be serious.

His lips flattened. "I'd never want to hurt you like that. But what else can I do? I was made to be a firefighter but the thought of hurting you like Jason…"

"Jason never had the power you do." She

squeezed her eyes tight at the admission. At what the words meant.

Omar laid a hand on her forearm. "What do you mean by that?"

She peered at him. "Can we just forget I said that? Talk about something else? Or better yet, let's talk tomorrow." When she could get a better grip on her emotions.

"I know things have been a little weird between us, Trinity, but please, level with me." He folded his arms across his chest. "Tell me what's bothering you. *Be honest.*"

"You!" she shouted. "The thought of you rejecting me. That's what hurts." She hated the pain in her voice, but more, the words that hung between them.

She wasn't ready to confess her feelings, hadn't built her armor back up or erased her fear enough to have this conversation.

Omar shifted. "I don't know what you want me to say."

Her breath shuddered and tears sprang to her eyes. "I shouldn't have to tell you what to say. Weren't you the one talking about honesty?"

He dipped his head, shoulders slumped.

This was it. He didn't love her.

She'd always be his friend, but right now, she wanted to be his wife. A *real* wife. "I'll be at my mom's house."

* * *

At her words, a piercing ache ripped through his insides. "For how long?"

Surely, she was coming back. She only needed a breather and not a permanent change of residence like he feared.

"Until…" Her voice got soft and she shrugged.

He should have said what he'd wanted when she mentioned being rejected. That it was the last thing on his mind to do. How much he loved her. But instead, he'd frozen as his mind played over the fact that death was a possibility in his job, as she'd pointed out. That he could try to save another and lose his own life, making her a widow.

Hurting her in a way he'd never want to.

Why was life so complicated?

He wanted nothing more than to live happily ever after with his best friend, the woman who'd melted his heart and brought light back into his life—into his children's lives. Faith and Joy had blossomed under Trinity's love, but as cheesy as it sounded, so had he.

She let out a long sigh, full of heartache. "I'll be back before dinner, Omar."

He gulped. "Okay."

She strolled away from the rocking chair and down the steps, headed for her parents' house. He watched as she knocked on their door, feeling like a part of him was missing. Trinity wanted more than he could give. He didn't want to be selfish in love, but sacrificial. And surely, thinking of only himself and how she made him feel while disregarding the real hurt he could bring her by dying was wrong.

He was no longer scared of losing his heart to Trinity. It had already happened. With every bout of laughter and joy she'd brought into the home, his walls had crumbled and his heart had beat with joy once more. But if he were to die, to leave her, she'd suffer the same fate he had. The one that Rock was going through.

If you could have seen that Christine would die when she did, would that have stopped you from asking her out?

Rock's words reverberated in his mind. All this week, Omar had asked himself the question, mulled it over in his head. He finally understood why he'd had such a tough time answering it. For Omar, it was a no. Knowing Christine would pass wouldn't have prevented him from pursuing her or living the life they'd created. It was one that had blessed him immensely.

But he couldn't make that decision for Trinity. She deserved a choice, and by marrying for convenience, he'd taken that option away from her. They'd agreed they'd stay married and not even think divorce.

But she still has the option to love.

Did she? Did they still have an opportunity to make a go of their relationship the way God had intended? With love the source of all their actions? By not admitting his feelings, was he taking away another choice?

God, show me what to do. If I tell her I love her now, will she believe me?

Because he'd essentially rejected her when he'd stayed mute.

"Daddy? Mommy?"

Omar looked at the baby monitor. Sounded like Faith was awake, which meant he'd have to figure out what to say to Trinity later. Hopefully he could straighten out the mess he'd created by the time she came back.

Chapter Twenty

Trinity sat quietly as her dad watched the base-ball game. It was nice hearing the normal sounds of announcers and her dad periodically inter-rupting their dialogue to argue or state his own opinion. His antics while watching a game had al-ways amused her. Today, however, it barely broke through her thoughts of Omar and his silence.

What do you want me to say?

She wanted a declaration of love. One that would say they were in this together and she didn't have to fear his rejection because she had his heart. Some variation of the poetic declara-tions that came in all of her favorite rom-coms.

Obviously life wasn't a movie, but it would make it so much easier if she knew a happily-ever-after was in store for her. Instead, she had to garner strength to go back into that house knowing Omar didn't feel about her the way she felt about him.

Her head dropped onto her knees and she exhaled. Exhaustion weighed her down from fighting her thoughts and emotions. Her heart felt tattered and bruised beyond repair.

How do I go on, Lord? How do I act as if my heart isn't breaking?

She didn't want the girls to see any difference between her and Omar. It was so very important that they knew they were loved and that the house was filled with happiness for them. Except she'd messed it all up by falling *in love*. Why couldn't she have just stayed in the friend lane?

"You're thinking awfully hard over there, baby girl."

Trinity sniffed. "Sorry, Dad. I didn't think you'd hear my thoughts over the game." She tried for a smile but knew it fell short.

"You and your husband have a fight?"

She shook her head.

"Then what's got you so upset?"

"I love Omar." She blew out a sigh as sad as a deflated balloon.

Her dad's rumble of laughter drew her head around. She was pretty sure a fly could zoom right on into her mouth judging by the shock jolting through her body. "Why is that so funny?"

"Baby girl, you act like I have no clue as to

who you are. How you think." He speared her with a raised eyebrow. "Come on now."

"But that doesn't explain why you'd laugh."

"I knew your plans would get a good dose of reality." He winked. "That's why I'm laughing. Any time a person thinks they can control a situation and dictate the narrative, I simply shake my head and chuckle a bit."

"Daddy."

"What?" He smiled. "You can't be surprised that your heart would be the first to wreck your plans."

Maybe he saw the writing on the wall, but the shock was very much real for Trinity. "I am surprised."

"You know I was friends with your mother before we dated, right?"

She nodded, remembering the stories her parents had shared with her over the years. She'd always thought it was so dreamy they'd been friends and that their romance developed into more.

"But Omar had Christine."

"It's man who puts a limit on love, thinking if you've had one shot that there are no more blessings in store. I'm sure Omar thought Christine would be his one and only. Again, that's man planning and God showing us reality."

She shook her head. "Omar doesn't love me."

"Baby girl, you can't believe that."

"It's true. He told me."

"He said *I don't love you*?"

Well, no, but his silence spoke volumes. Hadn't it? "He didn't say those exact words." Her mind stuttered on that realization. Did it mean anything?

"Well, what *did* he say?"

"Nothing, Dad. Nothing." Her breath hitched as the memory brought a fresh wave of pain.

"Maybe he's being just as cautious as you. Y'all've been through a lot. Tends to make a person think before rushing in. Often think *too* much, if you ask me."

Trinity bit her lip, mulling her father's words over in her mind. Had she been too cautious? Too hesitant when she should have acted a little braver, bolder? Was Omar wondering those same things?

"How can you just make the switch? I've been so intent on protecting myself. I don't know how to just let that all go and figure out when it's time to be brave."

"Simple—trust in what God's doing in your life. You're so different today than you were when Jason abandoned you. Surely you see that, baby girl?"

She did. But how much of that was her wanting to be healed versus actually *being* healed.

"Get out of your head, Trinity Young, and trust your heart. God's been healing you and I believe

He's blessed you with a real chance at a life of love. There's been no pretense between you and Omar. Y'all knew what you were getting into." Her father chuckled again. "As much as a person can guess at."

"True. I didn't expect to fall in love."

"A God blessing for sure."

She smiled at her dad. She'd been looking at it all wrong. Thinking she had to keep her heart safe from hurt. Thinking that falling in love with Omar was the wrong thing to do. When all the while God wanted to give her a gift.

"What do I do now, Dad?"

He reached over and squeezed her hand. "Go home and enjoy your blessings."

She could certainly do that, but something told Trinity she needed to do just a little bit more than that. Maybe a declaration could happen after all.

Dinner had been tense. Omar had hoped to talk to Trinity while they readied the girls for bedtime, but Faith and Joy had both been intent on chatting about the latest Disney movie. Now that the house was silent as his girls slept, he fully intended on begging Trinity to talk to him. Only it looked like she'd disappeared.

A peek out front showed the front porch devoid of her presence, and the backyard was empty as well. He didn't think she'd retire so early, but maybe the stress of the day had exhausted her. He'd thought about knocking on her door, but a sense to be still and wait pricked his insides.

He didn't know if the feeling was a prodding of the Holy Spirit, but he would heed the thought and continue to lie in his room while praying for his marriage. Praying extra never hurt and could only help them.

Sometimes he marveled at how Trinity had become so much more than his best friend. They'd always been able to talk and understand one another beyond words, which was probably why the silence between them got under his skin so badly. He needed to know they would be okay. That they could move forward, together, as a family and as true husband and wife.

He closed his eyes, willing his mind to shut off. Perhaps if he gave in to sleep, joy would be waiting for him in the morning like the psalmist proclaimed. His cell phone chirped with an incoming text. He grabbed it off the nightstand, unlocking it with a swipe and hitting the text icon. His mouth dropped in shock as he saw a notification from Trinity.

Meet me at the tire swing.

Omar shot up, stopping to wince as his ribs protested the sharp movement. He blew out a breath as the pain eased, then stood at a more sedate pace. He slid his feet into flip-flops and headed downstairs. Thankfully he always slept in a T-shirt and exercise shorts. He never knew when the girls would wake up and need him in the middle of the night.

The text had to mean Trinity was finally ready to talk, right? Maybe now he could share all that was on his heart and prove to her he had the words. The right words that would hopefully change their relationship for the better.

He paused at the front door, saying a quick prayer before opening it and stepping outside. He should have grabbed one of the baby monitors, but maybe Trinity had thought of that already. The shock of her text had pushed it from his mind and, he had to admit, he was a bit too impatient to run upstairs now to get one.

Omar walked down the porch steps and headed next door toward the tire swing. He looked up and his steps slowed to a stop at the sight before him. The tree had been wrapped in white lights, and their glow beckoned him, urging his feet forward once more. His eyes flitted to the vision beside the tree, where Trinity stood in the red dress she'd worn to the justice of the peace. His breath suspended as his heart hammered in his chest.

This was a good thing, right? *Right, Lord?*

He gulped and closed the distance between them.

"Hi." Her smile was tentative, and her eyes squinted with nerves.

"Hey." Omar cleared his throat. "What's all this?" He gestured to the lights, his brain on autopilot as his thoughts went strangely quiet.

"Well, the swing has always been special to us." She peeked at him and then rushed on. "So, I figured this was the best place for me to say what I have to say."

He slid his hands into his pockets, hoping to hide the anxiety that had his stomach knotted up tighter than a box of electronic cords. "Go ahead."

"Omar, I'm sorry." Her lips turned downward. "I should have never shut you out like I did. You kept asking me to talk to you, and I just couldn't. I let fear keep me quiet and keep me from saying what I needed to say." Her shoulders rose and misery filled her eyes.

"Hey." He stepped forward. "There's nothing to forgive. I was doing the same thing. And you still said more than I could." He squeezed her hand.

"Really? You're not upset?" she whispered.

"You know I can't stay mad at you. You're my best friend." And hopefully would be more.

"Forever?"

"Forever."

Her lips tipped in a smile and his heart hammered as he waited. Did she have more to say?

She wouldn't light up their swing for a mere apology, would she?

Trinity exhaled a shaky breath, her lips quirking to the side. "There's one more thing."

"Just one?" And was it the big one? The one he'd been praying for since lying under the collapsed roofing?

"Yes, hopefully it's better than the apology."

"Well then, I'm all ears." Although it felt like the sound of his heartbeat had taken over that sense.

She smiled and closed the distance between them, winding her arms around his neck. Slowly the tension drained from his shoulders as her scent wrapped around them. He laid his forehead against hers. *This.* Right now, in this moment, he didn't care what else she wanted to say. He was just happy to have her in his arms, hoping that meant she'd let him into her heart.

Omar cupped her waist, and his eyes slid closed. Their feet shifted and he began to sway to the imaginary music.

"Why are we dancing?" she asked softly.

"Just seemed like a natural thing to do." He shrugged. "That and I'm happy you're in my arms."

"It's where I want to be."

"Do you?"

"Always."

He nuzzled the side of her neck, loving the lightness that filled his heart.

"You're distracting me."

Omar chuckled. "From what?"

"The last thing I wanted to tell you."

"I'm still listening."

"Are you?" she whispered in his ear.

"I am."

"Then hear this, Omar Young. I love you. Yesterday. Today. And tomorrow."

"Thank You, God," he breathed. "I love you too."

She halted, pulling back. "You do?"

He chuckled. "I figured this light display meant you knew."

"No. It's my declaration." She grinned, a dimple flashing with pleasure. "I mean, I'd hoped."

"Well, rest assured. I love you, pretty much have known since after the accident." He brushed her braids behind her shoulder. "I was just too scared to say anything."

She groaned. "How much time have we wasted because we gave in to fear?"

"Too much."

"And you're not afraid now?" She eyed him. "You didn't seem to know what to say earlier."

He hunched up a shoulder. "My mind was processing a little slowly." He cupped her face. "But it's not now. I love you, Trinity. And *not* as just a friend either."

She grinned. "As a husband loves his wife?"

"Exactly."

"Perfect." A thoughtful look came into her gaze. "Omar, I just want you to know that if fear rises up once more, if it knocks on my door, I won't let it rule me."

"And I promise to do the same."

He closed the gap between them and kissed her, so thankful that all was right between them. He didn't know what tomorrow would hold, but as long as Trinity loved him, he knew they would get through anything life threw their way.

He stepped back. "Let's go home."

Epilogue

June 7th, a year later

"You look stunning." Trinity's mom squeezed her shoulders, standing beside her as they gazed into the full-length mirror.

"I feel stunning." She smiled at her reflection.

The fit-and-flare gown was covered with beautiful, intricate lace, complete with an illusion neckline. The dress was everything she'd imagined and more. Best of all, the wedding gown made her as happy as the first day she'd tried it on.

Trinity still couldn't believe Omar had asked her to marry him. *Again.* The proposal at their swing had meant so much, and now, the tire swing had been cemented as their way of marking important events. Somehow, her parents had figured that out because they'd moved it from their tree to the one on the Young property for their anniversary gift.

She looked at her mom. "This has been such a good year, Mama."

"I'm so happy for you two." Her mom dabbed at her eyes with a handkerchief.

"Thank you. Your support has been a huge blessing to us."

She thought her parents would have a rough time seeing Omar as a true husband versus her best friend. Turned out, she'd been wrong. Her parents had been praying for a love match since they'd said *I do* the first time.

Omar and she were experiencing their sweet spot. Life with the girls was good. Rock had been visiting more and more. She was glad that the shadows around her honorary father-in-law's eyes didn't seem to be as dark as they'd been last year. She knew he still missed Nancy, but he'd found moments of joy since.

Her mom sniffed, nodding as she tried to hold in her tears.

Trinity smoothed a hand down her abdomen, turning to the left then to the right. The dress really was stunning. "You know it's a good thing we're having the ceremony on our anniversary."

"Why's that, sweetie?"

She paused. "Because in a couple of months, I won't be able to fit into this dress anymore. That would have been a big waste of alteration money." She met her mother's gaze in the mirror, waiting for her to catch the clue.

Her mom's mouth dropped open. "Oh, Trinity. Really?"

"Yes, ma'am. You'll have a new grandbaby the beginning of February." The pregnancy test she took yesterday had confirmed her belief, and already Trinity had been dreaming of holding a little boy.

"Oh, Trinity." Her mom covered her mouth, shoulders shaking as tears collected at the corners of her eyes.

"Mama, you're gonna ruin your makeup. Guess I should have waited until after the ceremony to tell you, huh?"

"Oh you." She dabbed at her eyes. "I'll fix my makeup before your father comes in to walk you down the aisle."

"I'll let you tell him."

"You know I will." Her mama winked, a huge smile on her face.

A knock sounded on the door and her father peeked his head around it.

"Come on in, Daddy."

He smiled as he walked all the way into the room. "You look beautiful, baby girl."

"Thank you."

"You ready?" He held out his arm.

"So ready." She placed her hand in the crook of his elbow.

The first time around, Trinity hadn't missed having a wedding ceremony. Truthfully, she'd been too nervous and full of painful memories to enjoy the moment of marrying Omar. But now, after everything they'd been through and the love shared between them, well, she knew this ceremony would be absolutely perfect.

Thank You, Lord.

Trinity took a step through the church's double doors and her breath caught. The naked adoration on Omar's face had her holding back tears. This time, she couldn't contain her smile as they said their vows. Standing before friends and family, especially the girls and Jalissa as her maid of honor, somehow made life all the sweeter. She knew this ceremony was only to cement the love they had and to recognize the power of vows said before God. They didn't need it to continue honoring one another. Nevertheless, it felt like a brand-new start.

* * * * *

*If you enjoyed this book,
pick up these other
sweet romances from Love Inspired.*

Someone to Trust
by Patricia Davids

Her Forbidden Amish Love
by Jocelyn McClay

Choosing his Family
by Jill Lynn

His Dry Creek Inheritance
by Janet Tronstad

A Home for Her Baby
by Gabrielle Meyer

*Find more great reads at
www.LoveInspired.com*

Dear Reader,

Thank you so much for reading Omar and Trinity's story.

Marriage of convenience stories happen to be my favorite trope. There's something about a marriage of convenience story that tugs at my heartstrings. The uncertainty of what their future will look like—even if they've known their spouse for a long time, as Omar and Trinity had. Watching and waiting for them to find common ground and get to the happily-ever-after. Throw in two precious toddlers and you have a recipe for great story fodder.

I loved bringing Omar and Trinity together as they healed from past wounds and learned to let promises of God steer them to happiness. I imagine they'll have many years of happiness ahead of them.

I would love to connect with you. You can find me on Facebook at www.Facebook.com/authortonishiloh or find me on my website, http://tonishiloh.com.

Blessings,
Toni

Get 4 FREE REWARDS!

We'll send you 2 FREE Books plus <u>2 FREE Mystery Gifts.</u>

Harlequin Heartwarming Larger-Print books will connect you to uplifting stories where the bonds of friendship, family and community unite.

FREE Value Over $20